DUDLEY PUBLIC LIBRARIES

The loan of this book may be renewed if not required by other readers, by contacting the library from which it was borrowed.

KT-405-632

THE
PORRIDGE OF
KNOWLEDGE

000000954919

ALSO BY ARCHIE KIMPTON

Jumblecat

ARCHIE KIMPTON

THE PORRIDGE OF KNOWLEDGE

ILLUSTRATED BY KATE HINDLEY

HOT
KEY
BOOKS

First published in Great Britain in 2015 by Hot Key Books
Northburgh House, 10 Northburgh Street, London EC1V 0AT

Text copyright © Archie Kimpton 2015
Illustration copyright © Kate Hindley 2015

The moral rights of the author and illustrator have been asserted.

All rights reserved.
No part of this publication may be reproduced, stored or transmitted
in any form by any means, electronic, mechanical, photocopying or
otherwise, without the prior written permission of the publisher.

All characters in this publication are fictitious and any resemblance to real
persons, living or dead, is purely coincidental.

A CIP catalogue record for this book is available from the British Library.

ISBN: 978-1-4714-0280-7

1

This book is typeset in 11pt Sabon using Atomik ePublisher

Printed and bound by Clays Ltd, St Ives Plc

MIX
Paper from
responsible sources
FSC® C018072

www.hotkeybooks.com

Hot Key Books is part of the Bonnier Publishing Group
www.bonnierpublishing.com

For Rogs, who showed me how to skacz

DUDLEY PUBLIC LIBRARIES	
000000954919	
£5.99	JF
04-Jun-2015	PETERS
JFP	

CHAPTER 1

MISSING

Grandad was missing. It was the third time this month he'd gone missing; the fourth if you counted the time Milk found him snoozing in his armchair, buried under a pile of old newspapers. But that didn't really count as *missing*, because on that occasion he hadn't even left the house.

Milk put on her coat, went outside and looked up and down the road. Grandad had such a distinctive walk you could see him coming from a long way away. He had a long, lolloping, flat-footed stride, shoulders slightly hunched and his arms dangling by his sides. He always moved slowly and steadily like a creature from the swamp – well, that's how a neighbour, Mrs Frat, once described him. And she meant to be unkind.

Seeing nothing, Milk reached up and rang the large brass bell that hung outside her front door – three hefty clangs.

A minute passed and then, one by one, her neighbours popped their heads out of their front doors.

'Has he gone missing again?' asked nice Mrs Farley. 'I've had a quick look around. He's not in my house.'

'I looked through all my biscuit tins,' wheezed old Mrs Fozz, who was a bit batty herself.

'Was he there?' asked Milk.

'Not this time, dear.' She waved a banana under Milk's nose. 'Do you want a banana? You look like you could do with a banana.'

'No thanks, Mrs Fozz. Maybe later,' smiled Milk. Mrs Fozz was always trying to fatten her up.

Mr Fub stuck his head out of his front door. 'Not here.' Mr Fub always sounded slightly annoyed, but it was just the way he spoke – gruff, like an old billy goat. 'Have you checked the beach?'

'Not yet. I'm going there now. Thanks, Mr Fub. Thanks, everybody.'

Milk started off down the hill towards the beach. After ten paces, she looked back over her shoulder. Mrs Farley and Mr Fub had gone back indoors, but as usual, Mrs Fozz was still standing on her doorstep, grinning from ear to ear and waving the banana high above her head. It didn't mean anything; Mrs Fozz was just funny like that.

Not all of her neighbours were as helpful. Halfway down the hill, Milk crossed the road and began walking just a little bit quicker, ducking her head down behind parked cars. But it was too late. She'd been spotted. Mr Frat yanked open his front door and marched out onto the street.

'Ringing that stupid bell at all hours,' he yelled across the road. 'I hate that bell. *And* you've interrupted *Massive Vegetables*. It's my favourite programme.'

Mrs Frat stepped outside and stood beside her husband. 'Your grandad oughta be locked up,' she growled, glaring at Milk. 'He's a menace, that's what. A useless old menace. What have you got to say about that?'

Milk had learnt some time ago not to discuss things with the Frats. It only made them shout even louder. On the other hand, she wasn't going to apologise either. 'OK,' she replied neutrally.

'OK? OK!' screamed Mr Frat. 'You interrupt *Massive Vegetables*, and, I might add, this episode is about massive turnips, which happen to be my favourite massive vegetable. And all you've got to say is "OK"?'

3

Two Frat children nervously poked their heads out of the door to see what was going on. Milk knew them from school. They were called Frank and Fenella and they hardly ever said a word, neither in the classroom nor on the street. On top of that, they always looked terribly unwell; pale and sniffly, with trails of glistening snot on their sleeves as if slugs had been using them as a mollusc motorway.

Milk waved at the children. 'Hi Frank. Hi Fenella.'

Hurriedly, Mrs Frat shovelled her children back indoors. 'Get back inside, you two,' she barked. 'I won't have you fraternising with the likes of her, whatever she's called.' She turned to her husband. 'What *is* she called? Something stupid like Egg or Cheese?'

'Milk. She's called Milk,' smirked Mr Frat.

'Ha! Milk!' Mrs Frat practically spat out the word. 'Well, that proves it. They're barking mad. Diseased! Brain diseased, the lot of them. No wonder her mother abandoned her. I would have done the same!' And with that she and Mr Frat stomped back inside, slamming the door behind them.

It was soon after Grandma died that Grandad had begun behaving a bit oddly – silly little things like brushing his teeth with butter or wiping his nose on the cat. Then, one day, he started wandering off, just getting up out of his armchair and going out without saying a word. At first, Milk would worry terribly and follow him. In those early days she even kept a diary of everywhere he went.

April 5th – Found Grandad in Mrs Fozz's house, sleeping behind her sofa. When Mrs Fozz came back from the shops she was a bit surprised, but she didn't mind and gave us home-made chicken ice cream (not nice).

April 14th – Found Grandad dancing on the beach.

April 20th – Followed Grandad for ages. He stopped by the reservoir and talked to some cows. Seemed happy.

May 2nd – Mrs Fozz's house. Again! He likes it there. When Mrs Fozz came out of the shower she was a bit surprised, but she didn't mind and gave us home-made broccoli biscuits (not nice).

After a few weeks, Milk stopped following Grandad. There was no need. He never went too far and he never got into any trouble and he was perfectly safe when he crossed the road, so she didn't worry. He just liked wandering about and talking to people or animals or trees or lamp posts or lawnmowers or bins. Only occasionally, like today, did Milk actually go out and look for him. It was getting late and besides, he'd probably be getting hungry for his dinner.

At the bottom of the hill, Milk crossed the road onto the promenade. As usual, it was a damp and windy day in Slopp-on-Sea; the kind of day when the sky and the sea coalesced into one great, grey, gloomy splodge. Milk put up her hood and went over to her telescope. Some years back, the Mayor of Slopp-on-Sea had installed five of these coin-operated telescopes along the seafront wall. Nobody knew why. There was nothing to see; the pier, with its rusting Ferris wheel, had closed down a long time ago and the sea was always a dirty, sludgy colour.

Milk vividly remembered the excited crowd at the grand opening of the telescopes. She couldn't have been much more than four years old, but perched on her grandad's shoulders she felt ten feet tall.

'What can you see?' asked Grandma, looking up at Milk. 'Can you see the new telescopes?'

'Big ears,' replied Milk, joyfully flicking Grandad's ears.

'One day your ears will be bigger than mine,' teased Grandad.

'Nooo!' giggled Milk.

'They'll be so big you'll be able to fly to the moon.'

'Nooooooo!' she squealed, giving Grandad's lughole a hefty yank.

Just then the Mayor of Slopp-on-Sea tapped on the microphone. 'Good people of Slopp,' he announced pompously, 'it is with great pride that I declare these telescopes open.'

There was a slightly awkward moment as the blunt mayoral scissors refused to cut through the ribbon and the Mayor's assistant had to use her teeth to tear through it. Then, typically, nobody had remembered to bring 20p, so the Mayor couldn't even demonstrate how wonderfully *telescopic* the telescope was. Soon after, everybody went home and the telescopes were quickly forgotten.

These days, of the five telescopes, only one still worked, and apart from the occasional holidaymaker, Milk was the only person to use it. She felt beneath the tube of the telescope and found her 20p coin stuck there with old chewing gum. She peeled the gum off the coin and put it in the slot. There was a gentle *click* as the telescope activated. Milk put her eye up to the telescope and scanned the beach. Normally Grandad was quite easy to find. He had his favourite spots. Sometimes he liked to sit on the pebbles and stare out to sea. Other times he danced, jiggling about like an electrified chicken, conducting the grey skies with his hands. Nor was it unknown for Grandad to strip off all his clothes and go skinny-dipping. He was still a strong swimmer and sometimes Milk would spot his age-speckled bald head bobbing around in the water. But not today.

After two minutes there was another gentle *click* and the

view through the telescope went black. Time was up. Milk opened the coin box underneath the telescope and retrieved her 20p. A little spit, a roll and a squidge between her fingers and the chewing gum was as sticky as ever. She squished the coin back into the gum and stuck it back underneath the telescope, ready for next time.

She followed her usual route along the promenade; past the public tennis court, long since overgrown with weeds, and past Carp's Café, which had shut for the evening. That's when she saw him – the familiar lolloping figure heading towards her along the seafront. As ever, Grandad moved slowly and steadily, never in a hurry. Even from a distance Milk could hear him chattering to himself.

'Who were you talking to?' she asked, when they finally met up.

'Pirates. They wanted stamps. I was directing them to the post office.'

'But the post office closed down last year. Don't you remember?'

'Oh fiddlesticks,' replied Grandad. 'Well, it's too late now. They'll be halfway there already.'

'Anyhow, why would pirates want stamps?'

'Well, that's what I thought, but I didn't like to ask. Maybe they want to send a letter,' he said, scratching his head. 'Come to think of it, maybe they didn't want stamps at all. Maybe they said pants. Do they sell pants at the post office?'

'Maybe they wanted planks?' suggested Milk.

'That's the daisy!' yelped Grandad. 'Planks! They were

looking for planks. New planks. For walking on. That'd be it. Pirates are always walking the plank.'

'Well, I'm happy I found you and not the pirates,' said Milk, giving him a little hug.

'No, I found *you*,' replied the tall, old man. 'What were you looking for?'

'I was looking for you, Grandad. Are you coming home?'

'That depends on you. Are you going home?'

'Yes, Grandad.'

'Well, good. So am I then,' he said, beaming down at her. He set off at his slow, steady pace, Milk at his side.

'Oh, I almost forgot,' he said, reaching into his coat pocket. 'This is for you.'

He handed her a thin red book, the size of a postcard. It had a hard cover and was rather tatty, as if it had been left out in all weathers. Milk turned it over in her hands. Along the spine of the book, in faded gold letters, was written:

THE PORRIDGE OF KNOWLEDGE.

'Where did you get it from?' she asked.

'What?'

'This!' cried Milk, waving the book in his face.

'Oh, that. I was given it.'

'Who gave it to you?'

'What?'

'The book!'

'Oh, that,' replied Grandad. 'I found it on the beach.'

Grandad often found things, picked them up and then

forgot where he found them in the first place. A couple of weeks ago he came home with a small pancake draped over the top of his head. He didn't know how it had got there, but he couldn't stop giggling when Milk put him in front of a mirror.

Milk put the book back in Grandad's coat pocket, took hold of his hand and headed for home.

CHAPTER 2

BARRY THE MILKMAN

It was never a secret. Milk had always known what had happened to her when she was a baby. At the time it was front-page news:

BABY FOUND ON MILK FLOAT,

screamed the *Slopp-on-Sea Gazette*, adding,

MOTHER'S WHEREABOUTS UNKNOWN.

(The same front page also asked,

ARE MUSHROOMS MORE INTELLIGENT THAN PEOPLE?
A GAZETTE EXCLUSIVE,

but that really wasn't so important. And by the way, the answer is no, mushrooms are not more intelligent than people.)

11

For the first few months of her life, the abandoned baby was cared for by nurses in the hospital. For obvious reasons they called her Milk (well, they could hardly call her Barry, which was the name of the milkman who'd found her). It was Grandma, the senior nurse at the hospital, who suggested she look after the baby at home until a more suitable family could be found. So baby Milk went to live with Grandma and Grandad, and the days rolled into weeks and the weeks rolled into months and the months slipped by until one day, to everybody's delight, it was decided that Milk should stay with them forever.

They kept that front page of the *Slopp-on-Sea Gazette*. It was put in a frame and hung over the kitchen fireplace at home. Milk loved looking at it. It reminded her how lucky she was to end up living with her adopted grandparents.

You could say it was her destiny.

Grandad put another log on the fire and stepped back, brushing away a cobweb stuck to his fingers. Gradually, the kitchen filled with warmth and the soporific smell of burning wood.

'You could boil a blister in there,' he said, staring proudly at the fire.

'It's a beauty, Grandad. A proper blanket-blazer,' replied Milk, using one of his made-up expressions.

She cleared the dinner plates from the kitchen table and put them in the sink. This was their routine: Milk cooked then Grandad washed up and tidied away, though recently his tidying had become increasingly haphazard – clean plates sometimes ended up in the fridge and the butter dish might be left on the floor next to the cat's bowl. But still, he insisted on doing it and besides, the cat loved butter.

Grandad wheeled his armchair close to the fire, sat down and opened the newspaper: the *Slopp-on-Sea Gazette*. He never read it, he just liked to doodle, drawing donkey's ears on the mayor's head or scribbling moustaches onto the happy faces of the victorious ladies' wrestling team – that kind of thing. At the same time, Milk settled down at the kitchen table and took out her homework book, *You Love Maths, Maths Loves You*. She opened it at Chapter 6: *Number Hugs: Let long division fill your heart.*

Despite the heat from the kitchen fire, Milk shivered. Already, her brain was beginning to freeze over. This was perfectly normal. Homework, particularly maths homework, was one big brain-freeze.

Absent-mindedly, her eyes began to wander across the table, searching for something less mind-numbingly dull. There were piles of old comics, empty crisp packets, a takeaway menu for Carp's Café and there, next to a shrivelled banana skin, was the little red book that Grandad had found earlier today. Milk had forgotten all about it, but now, compared with her homework, it suddenly became more intriguing.

She opened the book and began to read.

It was a short story, written entirely in rhyme, about a medieval vagrant called Jim, who spent his days traipsing through villages, begging and stealing from whoever crossed his path. One day, Jim stumbled into a village, which was celebrating its annual Porridge of Knowledge festival. Looking for something to steal, Jim slipped into a tent and found a cauldron full of porridge. What he didn't know was that this was no ordinary porridge; whoever ate it, temporarily developed extraordinary powers. Greedily, he ate the whole lot before being caught in the act by the angry villagers . . .

The Porridge of Knowledge rolled down Jim's chin,
And carved a white trail on wine-cratered skin.
A thick yellow tongue then wormed from his mouth,
Went north, licked the top lip and then headed south.
But porridge still hung from his jaw and his whiskers,
Stuck to his dewlap, his boils and his blisters.
Encrusted as such he looked up at the crowd,
Who'd gathered around him, some silent, some loud,
Some angry, some praying to the god of all knowledge,
But most just stared at this man who'd had porridge.

'What are you reading?' asked Grandad, arching his head back to look at his ten-year-old granddaughter.

'The book you found.'

'What book?'

Instead of explaining all over again how the book had got into their house, Milk decided to read out loud. She continued from where she had left off, where Jim, covered in porridge, was confronted by the angry villagers . . .

'Jim grinned at the mob, his mind all ablaze
With fear and confusion and wine-addled haze.
And tried to look sorry, forced tears to his eyes,

*And begged for forgiveness with whimpering cries,
"'Twas only some porridge to soak up my wine.
What's the world come to if hunger's a crime?"'*

Milk stopped. Grandad was snoring loudly and somehow he'd managed to completely cover himself in freshly doodled newspaper. She fetched a blanket and laid it over him, removing the one sheet of newspaper that covered his bald head. He really was totally bald. Not a single hair grew anywhere on his head apart from the wiry strands that dangled out of his nose as if two tiny brooms had been shoved up his nostrils with the brush ends sticking out.

Thankfully, Milk was the opposite. No hairs hung out of her nose, and on top of her head grew a thick mop of chocolate-brown hair, cut into an unruly bob. She liked having a 'bob'. It made her think that she had a friend called Bob, who was always hanging out with her.

Only occasionally did she wonder if she looked like her real mother, the one who abandoned her on the milk float. But she never let it trouble her. In fact, nothing gave her greater pleasure than when people told her that she looked like Grandad.

'Aren't you getting tall, just like your grandad,' nice Mrs Farley would say.

Or Mrs Fozz might remark, 'You've got your grandad's ears. Nice and flappy.'

Of course everyone in Slopp knew that Milk was adopted and that any similarities to Grandad were just a coincidence, but still, to be told she looked like him was the best compliment she could ever wish for.

It took her less than an hour to read the rest of *The Porridge of Knowledge*. As you might expect, the roguish Jim got his comeuppance. Because he had eaten far too much porridge far too quickly, his head expanded and then exploded, splattering splodges of porridge from one side of the village to the other. Gruesome really, but no more so than some of the old fairy tales that Grandma had read to her when she was little.

She closed the book and stretched with the satisfied feeling that washes over you when you finish a good story. Not a great story by any means – she preferred her comics, with

their slap-bang-wallop daftness – but it had happily taken her away from her homework for a while. She pushed the remaining logs together in the fire and tucked the blanket around Grandad. It wasn't unusual for him to sleep all night in his armchair; in fact, he slept comfortably in any number of places. Not so long ago, Milk found him on the bathroom floor, curled up on a large cushion that the cat sometimes used. He was still there the next morning, except the cat had joined him, her furry body draped over his bald head, like a mother chicken protecting her egg.

Milk decided to do her homework in the morning before school. She stacked her schoolbooks into a pile at the end of the table, putting *The Porridge of Knowledge* on top. But books, like most things, don't always do what they're told. The little red book slid off the pile and landed, with a flutter of pages, on the kitchen floor. As Milk bent down to retrieve it, she noticed there were some handwritten words scrawled on the inside back cover.

It was a list of ingredients.

> *3 pints of water*
> *6 oz of oatmeal*
> *3 teaspoons of salt*

Of course, Milk knew these were the three basic ingredients needed to make porridge. Most winter mornings she made two steaming bowls of the stuff for Grandad and herself. But the recipe didn't stop there. In fact, it became decidedly weird . . .

8 slices of burnt toast (without crusts)
1 small pig's kidney
14 limp limpets
1 bar of cabbage soap
2 grapes
33 white blackberries
1 pea, quartered
6 tablespoons of dandruff

Milk smiled. Six tablespoons of dandruff! As if! Someone must have written the recipe in the back of the book as a joke. *Very funny*, she said to herself, rolling her eyes, because it wasn't very funny at all.

Without any further thought she put the book back on the table, kissed Grandad on his forehead and went up to bed.

Milk couldn't sleep.

Outside, the rain hammered against her bedroom window and the wind whistled over the roof like a tone-deaf ghost. However hard she tried not to, she could only think about the little red book. She had porridge on the brain.

She imagined the awful Jim guzzling down all the porridge. She pictured him as a small, weaselly man, with an abundance of dried snot caked beneath his nose. She wondered about the other children who might have read the same book, cheering at Jim's explosive end. *Ka-boom! Serves him right, the greedy guts.*

And then there was the recipe, handwritten on the back cover. It was a joke; of course it was. Limpets and dandruff in porridge? Ridiculous!

But despite all this, Milk already knew she wanted to try it out. Why not! Cook it up and see what happens. She would ask her friend Jarvis C. Carp to help. It'd be fun.

What possible harm could come of it?

CHAPTER 3

JARVIS C. CARP

The following morning, Milk left for school early. It was still raining and giant waves gushed and frothed onto the pebbled beach. She hurried along the promenade. The clouds were so low she could see only the vaguest outline of the pier. It looked like an unfinished drawing, without colour or detail, abandoned after just a few sketchy lines.

Carp's Café was the only shop on the seafront with its lights on. Milk peered in through the steamed-up windows. Already, Jarvis had written the day's menu on the blackboard above the counter. It read (and please note, Jarvis C. Carp's spelling was as bad as his cooking):

CARP'S STARTERS

Pienapple soup with garlick bred
Pienapple chunks with chese

21

* * * * *

CARP'S MAINS

Eel and spicy pienapple pie with mushed potatoe
Smoked lettice salad with pienapple chips

* * * * *

CARP'S PUDDOING

Happy pienapple surprise with chesey custard

Milk opened the café door. Immediately she was overcome by a sickly smell of burnt fruit.

'Jarvis?' she called out into the empty café.

'Is that you, Milk?' came Jarvis's voice from the kitchen. 'Come on through.'

The nicest thing you could say about Carp's Café was that the tea tasted only vaguely fishy and that the lettuce salad was quite, erm, *lettucey*. Other than that, the food was terrible. Atrocious! The omelettes tasted of rubber bands and the chips had been known to damage teeth. Even cockroaches thought twice about eating in Carp's Café.

Jarvis C. Carp, the chef and owner, tried to make good food, he really did. Every evening he watched cookery shows on television and his bookshelves were full of cookery books. But despite all this, his food remained revolting.

The trouble was that Jarvis C. Carp had no taste buds. He was born that way. He couldn't taste a thing. Zilch! And when you're a chef, that's a pretty serious drawback. As the old saying goes, a chef without taste buds is like a toilet without a flush.

To make matters worse, he had no sense of smell either, though this misfortune was entirely his fault. Aged nine, in a playground dare, Jarvis had shoved sixteen peanuts up each nostril – it was the school record! The doctor tried removing them with tweezers, but they just wouldn't budge. 'Give it a month and I'm sure they'll fall out of their own accord,' advised the doctor, adding, with a chuckle, 'Failing that, we can always use a pair of nutcrackers!' But they never did fall out and since that day, Jarvis hadn't smelt a thing. Not a whiff! As the old saying goes, a chef who can't smell is like a bath without a plug.

Milk crossed the café and parted the beaded curtain that divided the seating area from the kitchen.

'What do you think?' asked Jarvis proudly.

Milk didn't know what to think. Pineapples! Hundreds of them. Everywhere! On the surfaces, the shelves, in boxes on the floor and one in each of Jarvis's outstretched hands.

'They were going cheap at the market this morning, so I bought the lot. Don't you love pineapples? Doesn't everybody love pineapples?'

'Yes, but . . .'

'I made up some of the recipes all by myself. Look!' His fat little legs skipped over to the cooker, on which sat a large saucepan full of a gloopy, bubbling yellow liquid. 'Pineapple soup! And in here,' he pointed to another saucepan, 'is spicy pineapple sauce, to go in the eel pie. It's going to be incredible!' He plunged a spoon into the soup and held it out towards Milk. 'Try it. I'm sure it's delicious!'

Reluctantly, Milk took the spoon and sniffed the steaming liquid. Surprisingly, it didn't smell too bad. Milk shut her eyes and put the spoon into her mouth . . .

What a mistake! It was disgusting. More than disgusting. It was revoltingly disgusting. It tasted metallic and meaty, as if the pineapples had grown in tins of dog food.

'What do you think?' asked Jarvis. He was so excited his fat little legs twitched with enthusiasm.

Milk held the foul liquid in her mouth. She dared not swallow it. 'Is this one of your recipes?' she spluttered.

'No, no, no. I found this recipe in an old French cookery book. Do you like it? Oh, I'm so happy.'

Jarvis showed Milk the cookery book with a recipe entitled '*Soupe d'Ananas*'. Milk had learnt a little French at school, but only enough to ask where she might find her aunt's pen.

'My French is a little rusty,' admitted Jarvis. 'I know *ananas* means pineapple, the rest I guessed, but I got there in the end. It's delicious, isn't it!'

As Jarvis happily stirred the soup, Milk quickly spat the meaty-metallic liquid out of her mouth into the sink. She never told him that his food was terrible; Jarvis could be very sensitive and she didn't want to hurt his feelings. For instance, there was the time she suggested his cheesy sausages

were a little too cheesy and right away he closed the café for the rest of the day.

It was Milk's turn to ask a favour. She took the *Porridge of Knowledge* book out of her schoolbag and showed it to Jarvis. Quickly, for it was almost time to go to school, she explained the story of greedy Jim and how his head exploded after he ate all the porridge.

'And there's a recipe in the back,' she added.

Jarvis's eyes lit up. 'A recipe? Well, we must make it. Today!'

Milk had hoped he would say that.

'Does it need pineapples?' asked Jarvis, hopefully. 'Porridge with pineapples would be amazing.'

Milk shook her head. 'But it needs some pretty strange things.'

Jarvis ran his finger down the list of ingredients, nodding as he read each one.

'I know where to find limpets,' said Milk. 'I can go after school.'

'Leave the rest to me,' smiled Jarvis. 'I think I can get everything else.'

CHAPTER 4

PINEAPPLE BREATH

Ms Cerise moved up and down the classroom collecting homework books off each desk and dropping them into a wire basket she'd once stolen from a supermarket.

'I trust you've all done your homework. Not that I'm expecting much from any of you. Except for you, Reece. I'm sure yours will be excellent.'

An oily smile slicked across Reece Blanket's face as he handed over his homework. He was the new boy in the class and Ms Cerise had taken an instant shine to him.

'If only the rest of you could be like Reece, then we might actually achieve something in this classroom.'

Already Reece Blanket had earned the nickname 'Grease Blanket', though no one dared say this to his face, as he was by far the biggest boy in the class. Not yet eleven, he already had a trace of a fuzzy moustache sprouting above his top lip. Unfortunately for Milk, Reece sat right next to her at the back of the classroom.

'Boys like Reece are the reason I became a teacher,' continued Ms Cerise as she wiped clean the white board. 'Until he arrived I was beginning to wonder what on earth possessed me to become a teacher in the first place.'

Actually, she knew very well why she had become a teacher. Ms Cerise was a show-off. She loved showing off how much cleverer she was than anyone else. She had no interest in children or education or any of that nonsense; all she wanted was to be the cleverest in the room. Nothing made her happier than a pupil giving her the *wrong* answer. Then she would sit back in her chair, an awful, smug smile plastered across her face, just to let you know just how stupid she thought you were.

'Now then. Pie charts,' began Ms Cerise. 'Who can tell me what we use pie charts for? How about you, Fenella?'

As usual, Fenella Frat, the silent girl who lived on the same street as Milk, said nothing.

'What's that?' teased Ms Cerise. 'I didn't quite catch that. You'll have to speak up.'

Fenella slid down in her chair and stared at the floor.

'Hmmm, interesting. Perhaps your brother can help us. He's always so delightfully loquacious. Tell me about pie charts, Frank Frat.'

Frank sniffed and wiped his nose on his sleeve. He shifted uncomfortably in his chair, but like his sister, said nothing. At the back, Reece Blanket could barely contain his sniggers.

Ms Cerise was beginning to enjoy herself. Her eyes landed on Melanie Spoons.

'Ahhh, Melanie. Perhaps I should have come to you first. You look like you've eaten a few pies in your time.' Of course, Ms Cerise was referring to Melanie's size, which was extra large.

Just then, Reece Blanket raised his hand. 'Miss?'

'Yes, Reece?' asked Ms Cerise, beaming back at him. 'Do you wish to enlighten your dimwit classmates about pie charts?'

'I don't want to sit next to Milk.'

'Who would?' cackled Ms Cerise. 'She's only got half a brain. Semi-skimmed, I say.'

'It's not just that,' continued Reece. 'Her breath stinks. I can't concentrate.'

Milk felt the colour rise up into her face. To be humiliated by Ms Cerise was one thing. But to be humiliated by Grease Blanket, of all people, was almost more than she could tolerate.

'Is that so!' said Ms Cerise, licking her lips at the prospect of embarrassing Milk. 'And tell me, Milk, did you forget to brush your teeth this morning?'

'No.'

'Excuse me?'

'No . . . Ms Cerise,' said Milk through gritted teeth.

'Come up to the front, please.'

Slowly, Milk got up from her chair. Out of the corner of her eye she could see Reece Blanket grinning at her like a wasp at a picnic.

As Milk approached the front, Ms Cerise addressed the class. 'In my thirty-six years as a teacher I have learnt two things. Firstly, stupid children will always be stupid and though it breaks my heart, there is precious little I can do about it. Secondly, there is no excuse for poor personal hygiene. Reece, will you stand, please.' Obediently, Reece got to his feet. 'Everybody, look at this boy. Look at his shiny shoes and his beautifully combed hair. Show us your fingernails, Reece.' Reece extended his hands towards the class. 'See how they glisten like jewels. Fingernails are works of art, not tools to excavate nasal passages, Fenella Frat.'

'I always use a handkerchief, Miss,' boasted Reece, proudly pulling one out of his jacket pocket. 'And I brush my teeth four times a day. My daddy owns a toothpaste company.' Just to prove it, he opened his mouth wide and showed the class his perfect, sparkling gnashers.

'Thank you, Reece. You may sit down. Of course, I don't expect you all to be like Reece here. I'm not some kind of tyrant.' Ms Cerise turned to face Milk. 'But some of you seem to find it almost impossible to carry out the most *basic human functions*. Milk, open your mouth please.'

Ms Cerise brought her nose to within an inch of Milk's mouth. At this proximity Milk could see the thick layers of white make-up that Ms Cerise trowelled across her face and her lipstick, cherry red, exaggerating her thin, cracked lips.

'I won't ask you again. Open – your – mouth.'

There was only one thing for it. Milk took the deepest breath imaginable, opened her mouth and exhaled as heavily as she could towards Ms Cerise's nose.

As if punched by an invisible force, Ms Cerise stumbled backwards and collapsed into Melanie Spoons's lap.

'Urgh! Wh-wh-what is it?' she stuttered, melodramatically resting her hand on her brow like a fainting heroine.

'Pineapple soup,' answered Milk defiantly. 'It's on special today at Carp's Café. You should try it, Miss.'

For the first time that day the classroom filled with laughter. Even Frank and Fenella Frat managed a squidgy giggle.

'Silence!' squealed Ms Cerise, trying to regain her composure. 'All of you be quiet!' With some difficulty, she extracted herself from Melanie Spoons's lap.

'Milk! Get out of my class. NOW!'

'What about the pie charts, Miss?' asked Milk, innocently.

'Stuff the pie charts. What do I care about pie charts? GET OUT!'

As she made her way to the door, Milk turned and winked at Reece, the only one in the class without a smile on his face.

CHAPTER 5

ELEPHANT STONES

Milk never *tried* to get kicked out of Ms Cerise's class, though every time it happened, she couldn't help feeling an enormous sense of excitement. It was different to the normal days off school, like weekends and holidays, when the days merged leisurely into one another. On days like today she felt that every moment was tinged with possibility and that something magical was always just around the corner.

She ran home and quickly changed out of her school uniform. In the kitchen, she opened a drawer and took out a penknife given to her by her grandma on her fifth birthday. It wasn't a fancy penknife with nail files and turnip peelers, but one with a single blade that folded neatly into a wooden handle. In tiny handwriting, Grandma had engraved the words '*To whittle the hours away*' along the length of the handle. It was Milk's most treasured possession and every time she ran her finger across the wooden handle it reminded her of Grandma's wicked laugh and warm, sparkly eyes.

With the knife safely in her pocket, she went outside and started off down the hill. As she passed Mrs Fozz's house, the old lady herself opened her front window.

'In case you're worrying, Milk, your grandad's in here with me. We're playing hide and seek. He's very good at it. Goodness knows how he squeezed himself into my fridge. It took me twenty minutes to find him and only then because I needed a glass of prune juice. Almost gave me a heart attack when I opened the fridge door!'

'Thanks, Mrs Fozz. He loves it at your house.'

'It's no trouble at all, dear. Better than watching *Britain's Ugliest Pets* on the television.' And with a giggle she closed the window.

Further down the road, Mr Frat was standing outside his house smoking a cigarette.

'Kicked out of school again?' he sneered.

Milk ignored him and kept walking.

'If my Frank and Fenella get any ideas off you . . .'

'Who are you talking to?' boomed Mrs Frat's voice from inside the house. 'Get inside! *Britain's Ugliest Pets* is starting.'

Mr Frat flicked his cigarette into the street and slammed the door behind him.

It was half an hour's walk to the Elephant Stones, a series of massive, jagged boulders that millions of years ago had come away from the cliff and tumbled into the sea. When the tide was low, it was possible to climb up onto the first stone and jump from boulder to boulder, zigzagging your way quite some distance out to sea. It was fierce out here; the muscular wind always threatened to blow you off balance and toss you into the raging water.

It was Grandad who first brought her out onto the Elephant Stones. She was just a little girl at the time, but together they skipped fearlessly from boulder to boulder.

'Keep your head down,' he used to shout over the din of the crashing waves. 'That way the wind won't blow you away.'

And Milk would do as she was told, ducking down, following in his footsteps, memorising the best routes.

That was some years ago now, when Grandma was still alive and Grandad was less befuddled. Things were different now.

Lying down, curled over the edge of the furthest boulder, Milk stretched her arms towards a lumpet of limpets. In one hand she held her knife; around the other she had tied a plastic bag to put the limpets in. Below her, the sea roiled and roared as the endless waves smashed against the underside of the boulder, spraying seawater high up into the air. Milk's face was already soaked and the salty seawater stung her eyes, but still she edged forward, her hands getting closer to the large limpets. There were smaller limpets that were much easier to reach, but Milk ignored those; the Porridge of Knowledge recipe specifically asked for *limp* limpets, and in her mind, only large limpets could ever be limp.

'Large limp limpets. Large limp limpets,' she repeated to herself, faster and faster, making up her own tongue twister. Somehow, it helped her concentrate.

Inch by inch, Milk slid the tip of the knife down the rock face towards the first large limpet. She knew that if she accidently touched the shell before she was ready then the limpet would instinctively flinch and glue itself so tightly to the rock face that it would be almost impossible to prise off.

'Large limp limpets. Large limp limpets . . .'

Then, in one swift movement she thrust the tip of the knife under the edge of the shell.

'Got it!' she said, quickly twisting the knife.

She peeled the limpet off the rock and dropped it into the plastic bag. One down, thirteen to go.

After nine limpets, Milk shuffled back onto the top of the rock to inspect her haul. Her arms were getting tired and her wet hair clung to her face. She took the largest limpet out of the bag and, with the knife, scooped the gloopy flesh out of its shell. Then, turning the knife over, she rested the limpet flesh over the thick edge of the blade. In slow mollusc-motion, the limpet draped itself limply over the side of the knife.

'Perfect,' she said to herself. 'As limp as lettuce.'

The last five limpets were the hardest to reach, each one a little further down the rock face than the last. She worked quickly, stretching her body so far down she worried she might slide head first into the sea. Just as she prised off the last limpet she felt someone grab hold of her ankles. She arched her head back to see who it was.

'Saved you,' smirked Reece Blanket. 'Saved your life.' He was grinning like an idiot.

Milk ignored him. Cool as you like, she dropped the last limpet into the plastic bag and wiped her hair out of her eyes. 'Let go of me, Reece,' she said, calmly.

'When you're like this, I don't have to smell your breath,' giggled Reece. Now he was getting annoying.

'Get off me, Grease.'

'What did you call me?' snarled Reece, tightening his grip on her ankles.

Considering she was lying over the side of a boulder with her head just inches from the sea, Milk realised it probably wasn't a good idea to call him Grease again. Instead, she asked, 'Why aren't you in school? Did you get sent out as well?'

'Me?' Reece scoffed. 'As if! Ms Cerise sent us all home. She wasn't feeling well after you breathed on her. Now, let's see. What would happen if I lowered you over the edge? Just a little bit. Like this.'

Now Milk was dangling and the only thing stopping her falling into the water was Reece, holding onto her ankles.

'Reece,' yelled Milk, furiously. 'Pull me up. Now!'

A wave collided against the boulder, soaking Milk up to her waist. The plastic bag hanging from her wrist filled with seawater, dragging her down even further. It felt like her arm was being pulled out of its socket. All she could hear was the roar of the sea and Reece hooting with laughter.

'Say "I love Reece" or I'll drop you.'

Milk said nothing.

'You're getting heavy,' he trilled in a sing-song voice. 'I can't hold on much longer. You'd better say it, "I love Reece".'

He let her slide down even further. Milk could feel her hair touching the water. And then, disaster. The next wave smashed against her arm, knocking the knife out of her hand. Helplessly, she watched as it fell into the water and sank beneath the waves.

She'd had enough. 'I love Reece,' she growled through gritted teeth.

'What was that? I didn't hear you.'

'I LOVE REECE!' roared Milk furiously.

'There,' said Reece, pulling her up, 'that wasn't so hard, was it? I love you too. Let's kiss.' He puckered his lips in readiness.

Milk scrambled to her feet and barged past him.

Reece pulled a sad face. 'No kissy-wissy for Reecey? I only want to be your friend. It's not as though you have any friends at school.'

Milk hated to admit it, but Reece was right. At school she kept herself to herself. Nor did she ever ask anyone back to her house. These days her priority was to look after Grandad. That said, she wasn't desperate; it was better to have no friends than have Reece as a friend.

'Oh, by the way,' he called out after her. 'I wanted to invite you to my daddy's new café. It opens tonight on the pier. It's called Café Smoooth.'

Milk pretended not to hear . . .

'You should come.'

. . . but she did.

CHAPTER 6

THE INVITATION

Carp's Café had just two regulars. Their names were Alfred and Irene and they'd been coming to Carp's for as long as anyone could remember. Every day after lunch, they hobbled in, tucked their walking sticks under a table and sat down opposite each other. Then they'd order one cup of fishy tea, which they shared throughout the afternoon. For most of this time, unless they were sulking, they argued.

Today was no different. When Milk pushed open the café door she walked right into the middle of a real humdinger.

'Tell her, Milk,' fumed Alfred, pointing a shaky finger at Irene. 'Tell her she's wrong.'

'Oh, you're a miserable old fool,' hissed Irene.

Though they were the nicest of people, Milk never got involved in their quarrels. 'Hello you two,' she said breezily. 'Is Jarvis out back?'

'He's gone out, love,' replied Irene. 'He asked us to keep an eye on the place. Well, he asked me. Alfred here's as blind as a bat.'

'I am not,' insisted Alfred. 'I don't even wear glasses.'

'That's why you can't see, you old dingbat.'

'Well, at least I don't think Italians use *toothpasta* to clean their teeth. That's what she said this morning! Toothpasta!' shrieked Alfred triumphantly. He swept his long, unwashed hair away from his face and took a tiny slurp of fishy tea. 'I tell you, Milk, I should have her sent to the nuthouse.'

'You wouldn't last five minutes without me,' shot back Irene. This, they both knew, was true. Alfred and Irene were inseparable.

Only now did Irene notice that Milk was soaked. 'Oh dear, look at you. Come here. Sit down. What happened? Been wrestling whales again?'

'Something like that,' smiled Milk, taking a seat next to Irene.

'Well, I bet the whale came off worse,' chuckled Alfred. 'Here, put my coat on. Get yourself warmed up.'

Irene looked appalled. 'She doesn't want to be wearing that old rag. It's covered in dandruff. Here, put mine on.'

Just then the café door crashed open and Jarvis C. Carp stormed in, carrying a cardboard box under his arm. Without saying a word he dropped the box onto the floor and threw a screwed-up ball of paper on the table.

'What's that?' asked Milk.

Jarvis didn't answer. Whatever it was, he was very upset.

Milk unscrewed the paper and read out loud:

'PEOPLE OF SLOPP,
YOU ARE INVITED TO THE GRAND OPENING OF CAFÉ
SMOOOTH
TONIGHT AT 6 P.M. ON THE SLOPP-ON-SEA PIER.

FREE COCKTAILS
(FOR THE FIRST THREE GUESTS),
FREE SAUSAGES
(STRICTLY HALF A SAUSAGE PER PERSON)
AND FREE CAFÉ SMOOOTII PARTY HATS FOR ALL
CHILDREN UNDER TWO
(PROOF OF AGE REQUIRED, I.E. PASSPORT, DRIVING
LICENCE, ETC.).

SO . . .

GET OUT FROM UNDER YOUR DUVET
AND COME TO CAFÉ SMOOOTII.
EH!

(COACH PARTIES WELCOME)'

Jarvis collapsed onto the chair next to Alfred and buried his head in his hands. 'Ruined. I'm ruined,' he wailed over and over. 'Nobody will come here ever again.'

'We'll still come,' said Alfred, putting an arm around Jarvis. 'We love it here. Your tea is . . .'

'Fishy!' interrupted Jarvis. 'I know my tea is fishy. I heard you say so.'

'But that's how we like it,' insisted Irene, unconvincingly. 'I was just saying this morning how I'd love a cup of fishy tea, wasn't I, Alfred.'

Alfred nodded enthusiastically. 'And Jarvis, you mustn't forget about the holidaymakers. They'll still come.'

'You had a coach party today, didn't you?' asked Milk. 'How did they like your pineapple menu?'

Jarvis looked up at her. 'Three of them were sick, one couple refused to pay the bill and all of them left before I had a chance to serve the Happy Pineapple Surprise pudding. It was a disaster. It's always a disaster. I'm a terrible chef. They only eat here because there's nowhere else to go.'

'That's not true,' insisted Milk.

But it was true and they all knew it.

'What will I do? Maybe I'll have to close the café. Four hundred years of Carp's Café and it ends with me,' he sobbed.

Milk hated seeing her friend like this. She wished there was something she could do to make things better. On the floor, next to her bag of limpets, she noticed the cardboard box that Jarvis had dropped. In it, amongst other things, were oats, grapes, white blackberries and a piece of bloodied paper that probably contained a small pig's kidney; all ingredients for the Porridge of Knowledge.

'Right,' she said decisively, 'there's nothing else for it.'

She stood up, fetched a clean apron and pulled it over her head. It had 'World's Greatest Cook' written across the front.

'Are you coming?' she asked, standing over Jarvis.

'Where?'

'To the kitchen. We cook.'

CHAPTER 7

DANDRUFF

When he was a little boy, Jarvis dreamed of becoming an architect. While his mother and father ran the café downstairs, young Jarvis sat in his bedroom, sucking boiled sweets and reading his favourite book, *Great Buildings of the World*. They were all in there: the Taj Mahal, the pyramids of Giza, the Acropolis, the leaning tower of Pisa and his all-time favourite, the Eiffel Tower. They were his colourful world beyond the greyness of Slopp.

The very day Jarvis took over Carp's Café from his parents, he covered the kitchen walls with pictures of all his favourite buildings. It meant he could marvel at the Eiffel Tower as he washed up; he could gaze at the pyramids of Giza as he chopped onions, and as he waited for the toaster to pop, he could meander through the glorious arches of the Taj Mahal that glowed pink in the evening sun. These pictures inspired him and though they didn't improve his cooking one jot, he never stopped trying.

But now the kitchen was in total chaos. Spiky pineapple tops were all over the floor, piles of dirty plates lurked in the sink and somehow, three large chunks of pineapple had stuck to the picture of the Eiffel Tower. Milk got to work, washing, sweeping and cleaning. Meanwhile, Jarvis unpacked the contents of the box and laid them out in a neat row. Then he put a large saucepan onto the cooker and turned on the gas.

'Are you ready?' asked Milk, taking off her rubber gloves.

'Ready,' replied Jarvis.

They followed the recipe to the letter. First, the three basic ingredients of porridge: water, oatmeal and salt. Milk stirred as Jarvis prepared the other more unusual ingredients. Under the grill, he burnt eight slices of toast, cut off the crusts then slung them in the pot.

'Do I need to chop this up?' he asked, holding up the pig's kidney.

Milk consulted the recipe. There was no mention of slicing or chopping. 'Nope, just chuck it in.'

The kidney plopped in, settling comfortably on a bed of blackened toast.

Jarvis scooped the limp limpets out of their shells and dropped them into the pot. Then came the cabbage soap, two grapes and the thirty-three white blackberries, which he'd found growing in brambles near the Slopp-on-Sea reservoir.

It wasn't so easy to quarter a pea, but on his third attempt, having sharpened his best knife, Jarvis managed it.

'Voila!' he said with a flourish, tossing the quartered pea into the pot.

Stirring was hard work. Milk leant in and dragged the spoon around the bottom of the pot. 'Is that all the ingredients?' she asked.

'Yes, chef!' grinned Jarvis, clicking his heels together. 'Everything except the dandruff. I thought you could supply that.'

'I haven't got dandruff,' protested Milk.

'Well, don't look at me. I washed my hair last night.' It was true; Jarvis's hair was looking particularly fluffy, much like an Eighties pop star.

Milk touched her hair. 'Well, I'll try. But I'm sure I don't have dandruff.'

On the shelf by the beaded curtain was a pile of black paper napkins. Milk took one down and laid it flat on the kitchen table. Then, she leant over it and got ruffling.

Like the first snow of winter, a light dusting of dandruff floated down onto the napkin.

'Go on, scratch it!' encouraged Jarvis. 'Get behind the ears.'

Milk dug her nails in and scratched as hard as she could, but still there was nowhere near enough.

'Here. Let me have a go,' said Jarvis, leaning over the napkin.

He ruffled and fluffled but not a single flake fell out. It was a dandruff desert.

Milk picked up two corners of the napkin and tipped what they had into a tablespoon. It was less than half full.

'Where are we going to get six tablespoons of dandruff from?' asked Jarvis, resting his elbows on the table. 'Can you get it at the supermarket? It would be in the organic section, wouldn't it?'

Milk wasn't sure if Jarvis was joking, but she shook her head anyhow. Through the beaded curtain she could hear Alfred and Irene bickering – something about the time Alfred got his head stuck in a cat flap . . .

And then it came to her. Of course! It was obvious! 'Alfred?' she called out. 'Could you come into the kitchen please? We need your help.'

'Wee-hee!' cried Alfred, ruffling his dirty hair. 'It's snowing! A blizzard!'

Dandruff gushed down, turning the black napkin white.

'It's like Christmas,' said Jarvis, gleefully.

Irene was less than impressed. 'It's disgusting, that's what it is.'

By now, a healthy mound of dandruff rose up from the centre of the napkin. Milk tipped the contents into a bowl. There was more than enough.

'What do you need it for, anyway?' asked Alfred, putting his coat back on.

'It's nothing really,' replied Milk. 'Just a silly experiment.'

And really, that's all it was; a silly experiment. What was she expecting? To make porridge and become super-brainy? Even so, as Alfred and Irene said their goodbyes, Milk couldn't help wishing that something extraordinary might just happen. Whatever that *something* was, she had no idea. After all, it was just a wish.

CHAPTER 8

THE MOST TERRIBLE SMELL IN THE WORLD

Jarvis tipped the dandruff into the pot and stirred. It was sticky before, but now, with added dandruff, the texture was like glue.

'You try,' puffed Jarvis, passing the wooden spoon to Milk.

With two hands, she did her best, churning the mixture around the pot.

'How long do we have to cook it for?' asked Jarvis.

'It doesn't say. Let's get it simmering first and then . . .'

All of a sudden, the Most Terrible Smell in the World wafted up out of the pot and into her nostrils. Imagine putting your head into a bucket of used kitty litter. Well, it was nothing like that. It was worse. Seriously.

Milk gagged, pulling her jumper up over her nose. 'Oh my giddy aunt,' she exclaimed, using one of Grandad's expressions. 'It's disgusting.'

'What does it smell like?' asked Jarvis.

But Milk didn't need to answer. Her face, which was rapidly turning a shade of green, said it all.

The malodorous lump of gooey porridge began to bubble; plop, plop, plop, like lava splurting out of a sleepy volcano. Spirals of thick, foul smoke rose up, permeating throughout the kitchen. It was almost as if the contents of the pot had taken on a life of its own: a malevolent presence, a hideous cauldron of slop.

'This can't be right,' insisted Milk. 'We must have done something wrong. Look at it!'

The pig's kidney, which had shrivelled into a gelatinous, black blob, bobbed sluggishly on the surface of the porridge. Jarvis saw limpets clinging to the side of the pot as if they were trying to escape the stinking mixture beneath them. Though he couldn't smell a thing, Jarvis's useless nose somehow sent a signal to his brain that whatever was inside this pot was to be avoided at all costs. He looked at Milk. 'But we followed the recipe exactly as it was written. I don't understand.'

But Milk had had enough. 'It's a joke, Jarvis. And we fell for it.' She was annoyed with herself. 'Whoever wrote this recipe, if they could see us now they'd be laughing their heads off. I knew it was a joke the first time I saw it. I should have listened to myself. What a waste of time. I'm sorry, Jarvis.'

She pulled the apron over her head, flung it on the floor and marched out of the kitchen.

Milk sat in silence, skidding a large plastic tomato from hand to hand, back and forth across the table. It was bright red and had a green spout on the top for squirting out ketchup.

'Why don't we go and take a look at the new café?' suggested Jarvis. It was his turn to try and cheer up his friend. 'There's free sausages,' he added.

'Half sausages,' corrected Milk, grumpily.

Jarvis sat down at the table opposite her. 'If Carp's Café's going to survive, I want to know what I'm up against.'

'Do you really want to go?' asked Milk.

'Have you got a better idea?'

Milk looked towards the kitchen where the so-called Porridge of Knowledge lay festering. 'No. I don't suppose I do.'

Jarvis took the plastic tomato out of her hand and put it on the next table. 'Shall we go, then?' he asked, getting to his feet.

Milk sighed. 'OK, but we'll just look from the outside. I'm not going in. I don't want Grease Blanket seeing me there.'

'Who's Grease Blanket?'

'Nobody,' replied Milk, putting on her coat. 'He's nobody.'

CHAPTER 9

LAUNCH

The Café Smoooth launch party was already in full swing. Revolving spotlights shot brilliant beams up into the night sky and a three-piece band, all decked out in red-and-white-striped suits, played razzmatazz jazz, luring the people of Slopp onto the pier. Beside them stood a stilt-walker, as tall as a house, wearing a frothy-cup-of-coffee costume. His arms protruded from the sides of the giant coffee cup, patting passing children on their heads.

Milk and Jarvis stood on the other side of the road, in the shadows, watching the happy crowd thronging outside Café Smoooth.

'I've never seen anything quite like it,' Jarvis said flatly.

'Nor me,' replied Milk. 'Look at that boat.'

She pointed at an expensive-looking yacht that was moored alongside the pier. It was huge; large enough to house a swimming pool.

'It's like the whole village has turned up.'

'But they'll turn up to anything,' insisted Milk, trying to make things a little better for Jarvis.

She was right. Any event, however trivial, and the people of Slopp-on-Sea would turn up to have a look. Even a new road sign could draw a reasonable crowd. What else was there to do in Slopp? There was no cinema, no library; even the playground had recently closed down following a series of unfortunate accidents. (When the wooden see-saw collapsed, Fenella Frat was so badly splintered she couldn't sit down for a week.) 'Don't worry,' continued Milk, 'the fuss will die down soon enough.'

Jarvis smiled, but both of them knew that this was very bad news for Carp's Café.

Suddenly, from behind, a hand slapped down onto each of their shoulders.

'So nice of you to come,' smirked Reece Blanket, pushing himself in between them. 'I was beginning to think you might not make it. Have you seen our yacht? It's called the *Wet Blanket*. My daddy bought it two weeks ago. We live on it. I bet it's bigger than your house.'

With one arm firmly around each of their backs he began pushing them across the road towards the pier. For a ten-year-old boy, he was surprisingly strong.

'I'm afraid we don't have any pineapple soup on the menu today, but I'm sure you'll find something you'll like.'

'What are you doing, Reece? Get off me,' snapped Milk.

But Reece just tightened his grip and kept pushing. He wheeled them past the band, onto the pier, and before they knew it they were inside Café Smooth.

It was packed. Every table was full of excited customers tucking into ice creams, biscuits, cakes, hot chocolates with marshmallows and, of course, the complimentary half sausages. A queue snaked all around the sides of the café right up to a glistening stainless-steel counter, where six uniformed staff hurried back and forth, pouring tea, serving cake and expertly swirling patterns into the milky tops of frothy coffee. Everything was decorated in red and white stripes: the tables and chairs and walls and the ceiling and the coffee cups and the aprons and hats of the grinning staff. It was as if a giant tube of toothpaste had exploded and perfectly splattered the whole of the interior. There was even a massive fish tank at one end with a sad-looking dolphin swimming about inside. Just like everything else, the dolphin had been painted in red and white stripes.

'What do you think?' asked Reece.

'It's like toothpaste,' said Milk, deadpan.

'That's it!' beamed Reece. 'That's how Daddy made his money. Toothpaste! He made a fortune. And now he's branching out into cafés. This place is just the first. He's planning to build hundreds of Café Smoooths all over the country. He reckons that if people eat enough sweet stuff in his cafés, then they'll need to buy more of his toothpaste. Double your money. Brilliant, don't you think?'

Just then an enormous woman with a fountain of yellow hair stood up and bellowed across the café, 'Cooeee! Reecey, honey!' She wore a shimmering green and red dress that made her look like a plump watermelon. 'We're over here. Bring your little friends.'

'Coming, Mummy,' bleated Reece, pushing Milk and Jarvis through the crowds.

'Isn't it all wonderful!' exclaimed Mrs Blanket, clapping her hands together like a blubbery circus seal. 'So exciting. I'm already on my fourth slice of cakey-wake. And is this who you've been telling me about? Is this my Reecey's new girlfriend? Do you love my Reecey? Not as much as Mummy loves Reecey.'

Milk was horrified. What had Reece been saying?

Just then Mrs Blanket grabbed Milk by the waist and dragged her onto her lap. 'Now, let's take a proper look at you.' She clamped her hand around Milk's chin and yanked her head from side to side, examining her like a judge at a dog show. 'Well, for starters, we'll have to do something about your hair. Reecey likes long hair, don't you, Reecey? Extensions. That should do it. Lovely long hair, just like mine.' Mrs Blanket poked a fat finger into Milk's ribs. 'And she's a bit scrawny, but we can work on that. No time like the present.' And with that she scooped up a fistful of cake from her plate and shoved it into Milk's mouth. 'Other than that, you could be quite pretty. Don't you want to be pretty?'

Mrs Blanket wrapped her plump arms so tight around Milk's waist she could hardly breathe. 'Do you want a horsey ride, young lady? My Reecey loves horsey rides, don't you, Reecey?'

Milk tried to say, no thank you, she really, *really* didn't want a horsey ride, but her mouth was so stuffed full of cake she couldn't speak.

'Off we go then,' said Mrs Blanket cheerfully. She began jigging her legs up and down, singing, 'This is how the lady rides, clippity clop, clippity clop . . .'

Milk bounced up and down, her head flopping about like some loose-necked rag doll.

'This is how the gentleman rides, clippity clop, clippity clop . . .'

It was getting faster. Milk's stomach churned. She began to feel sick. She wanted to scream for help but only cake sprayed out of her mouth. Worst of all she knew what was coming next . . .

'This is how the farmer rides, clippity clop, clippity clop . . .'

She felt like a jumbled-up bag of bones riding a rickety rollercoaster that went on and on and on . . . until, with an enormous 'Weeeeeeeeee!' Mrs Blanket opened her legs and dropped Milk onto the red-and-white-striped floor.

'Wasn't that fun! Do you want another go?' giggled Mrs Blanket, scooping Milk back up onto her lap.

And then Mrs Blanket noticed Jarvis. 'And who is this *handsome* man? I'm Mrs Blanket. Lavinia. But you can call me Vinnie.' She extended a puffy, bejewelled hand towards him. 'And you are?'

Jarvis looked terrified. 'I'm J-Jar—'

'Speak up. I'm a trifle deaf,' trilled Mrs Blanket. 'Sponge in one ear. Custard in the other.' She roared with laughter at her terrible joke.

'I'm Jarvis,' spluttered Jarvis.

'Oh, how wonderful!' exclaimed Mrs Blanket. 'I used to

have a dog called Jarvis. It died of obesity, poor sausage. And what do you do, Jarvis?'

'He runs that café on the promenade,' said Reece, butting in. 'The one I was telling you about.'

Mrs Blanket looked puzzled, puckering her lips like a bloated fish.

'You remember, Mummy. Pineapple soup!'

Mrs Blanket roared with laughter yet again. 'Oh, that's you! The pineapple soup man. How wonderful! What a hoot!'

Mrs Blanket grabbed hold of Jarvis's hand and held on tight. 'You must meet my husband,' she squealed. 'Seeing as you're in the same line of business. Malcolm! Malcolm! Look at what I've got here.'

She elbowed the man sat next to her, who was passing a bulging envelope to the mayor.

'Can't you see I'm busy?' he snarled, with his back still turned.

'But Malcolm. This delightful man here is Jarvis.'

Reluctantly, Malcolm Blanket turned and glared at Jarvis. He had a thin, oval-shaped face, over which he wore a pair of steel-rimmed spectacles. Without moving his head he looked Jarvis up and down. Eventually, he said, in a quiet, nasal voice, 'And why might this man be of interest to me?'

'He runs the *other* café on the promenade,' explained Mrs Blanket, still holding onto Jarvis's hand. 'And he has a very firm handshake too. You'd better be careful, Malcolm; I think Jarvis here has a crush on me.'

Apart from a slight twitch in his left eye, Mr Blanket didn't move a muscle. He just stared. And then, ever so slowly, his lips began to curl back to reveal the most incredible set of brilliant, pearly-white teeth. In his mind, he was smiling. But in all of Malcolm Blanket's life he had never once smiled naturally. He didn't see the point of it. Smiling was for idiots. It was only at his wife's insistence that he had *learnt* how to smile. 'It might be good for business,' she had told him. 'Put people at ease.' So he practised; for hours on end in front of a mirror, straining and gurning until he achieved what he thought to be the perfect smile. The actual result was . . . well, rather toothy and just a little bit frightening.

'You must be Carp,' he said eventually, still brandishing his teeth like an angry dog. 'I'm very pleased to meet you.'

Jarvis squirmed. It certainly didn't look as though Mr Blanket was pleased to meet him at all.

'How do you like my new place?' continued Mr Blanket. 'Did you know it can seat one hundred and twenty people at any one time? We can make over three hundred cups of coffee in an hour. And my team of bakers can produce six hundred cupcakes in one night, all light and fluffy for the holidaymakers the next day. And the mayor here has just agreed to allow coaches to park right outside Café Smoooth. Haven't you, Mr Mayor?'

The mayor quickly put the bulging envelope inside his mayoral robes. 'Nothing like a bit of competition, eh Jarvis?' he murmured sheepishly.

'My thoughts precisely,' hissed Mr Blanket. 'Nothing like a bit of competition to get the blood pumping. And may the best café win. Though I feel you might have an unfair advantage with your *specialist* menu. I hear your pineapple soup is, err, breathtaking.' A strange gargling noise emanated from the back of his throat, like a weasel being strangled. This was the closest Malcolm Blanket ever came to laughter.

Jarvis looked close to tears. He didn't know what to say. He felt as helpless as a small, scared child arriving at a big, new school.

At last, Milk extracted herself from Mrs Blanket's clasp, took Jarvis's hand and led him towards the exit.

'Come over any time you like,' boomed Mrs Blanket. 'We can start on those hair extensions. Tomorrow, if you like. Oh, you're going to look so pretty for my Reecey.'

CHAPTER 10

ADVANCED MATHS FOR REALLY CLEVER PEOPLE

The following morning, on her way to school, Milk knocked on the door of Carp's Café. The blinds were down and no light came from inside.

She knocked again, harder this time.

Nothing.

Milk stepped back onto the road and shouted towards the upstairs window. 'Jarvis! Are you there? It's me, Milk!'

Her voice echoed along the empty seafront, but Jarvis's face didn't appear at the window and the curtains remained tightly closed.

Milk ducked down the alleyway and tried the kitchen back door. It was locked. She banged on it. Nobody answered. She heard a faint scratching and scuttling coming from inside – but it was nothing really. She banged again, calling out Jarvis's name. A seagull, scavenging near the bins, flew up and hovered, waiting for her to go away. But otherwise everything was quiet.

* * *

At school, Ms Cerise was wearing her best dress, the one she had once stolen from a department store.

'You look nice today,' greased Reece Blanket.

'Thank you, Reece.' You would have seen her blush if it wasn't for the layers of white make-up caked across her face.

'Is it a special occasion?' asked Melanie Spoons.

'Well, for starters, it's Friday, which means tomorrow is the weekend and I won't have to see you lot for a couple of days.' She wasn't joking. 'And, if you must know, I've been invited for tea and cake by Reece's mother, after school today.'

Apparently, as Ms Cerise explained, she had gone to the Café Smoooth opening the previous evening. There she met Reece's mother and father.

'It's not hard to see where Reece gets his manners from. Delightful people, the Blankets. And Mrs Blanket has such wonderful style. If only my teacher's salary allowed it, I would dress just like her.'

Milk couldn't care less what Ms Cerise was wearing or where she'd been invited. Her mind was elsewhere. She looked out of the classroom window and tried to think what might have happened to Jarvis. He *always* opened Carp's Café in the morning, whatever had gone wrong the previous day. For instance, there was the time he accidentally put super-spicy chillies in a child's birthday cake. Or the time his pet hamster, Bernie, climbed into the oven. Mistaking it for a baked potato, he served cooked Bernie, with baked beans, to a German vegetarian. Every time these disasters happened, Jarvis would close the café there and then, vowing never to reopen. However, come the next day, without fail, he would always reopen, full of enthusiasm to make things better. This was what Milk most admired about Jarvis. His resilience. He was like a plateful of jelly; when he was shaken he could have a bit of a worry-wobble, but the next day he would always bounce back to his normal happy self.

'Am I boring you, Milk?' asked Ms Cerise, rudely interrupting her thoughts.

'Yes,' replied Milk, without thinking.

Instantly, Ms Cerise's face went deep purple, the colour of her hideous dress. 'You are a nasty little girl,' she snapped. 'After everything I do for you. For all of you! I am a woman of the world, a *teacher*. My job is to make you into better human beings, but you just spit it back in my poor, poor face.' Theatrically she collapsed into her chair, covered her face with her hands and pretended to cry.

Ms Cerise regularly put on performances like this. The class was used to it. Before she became a teacher, Ms Cerise wanted to be an actress. The four days she spent in drama school were the happiest of her life; at last she could show off as much as she wanted. However, on the fifth day she was caught, red-handed, stealing six *Seven Dwarfs* costumes from the drama school storeroom and was promptly kicked out.

'Why should I care?' she wailed. 'Every day I come into this classroom and give you one hundred and ninety-nine per cent. And what do I get back? Nothing.'

She reached into her desk drawer and took out a pile of books. 'Fenella Frat, come up to the front, please.'

Fenella wiped her nose on her sleeve and did as she was told.

'Hand out these books,' ordered Ms Cerise.

Again, Fenella did as she was told, going up and down the classroom, putting a book on each desk. Milk picked up her copy. It was a fat, grey book entitled *Advanced Maths for Really Clever People*, by Syd Thicke. Milk opened her copy and flicked through it. Page after page of equations, diagrams and mathematical problems loomed back at her. The book really was as advanced as the title suggested.

'If you refuse to listen to me in class, then you can teach yourselves at home,' went on Ms Cerise. A cruel grin twisted the corners of her mouth towards the ceiling. 'Over the weekend you will study chapters one, two and three of Syd Thicke's excellent book. First thing Monday morning I will be testing you on what you have learnt. If any of you fail this test, I will do everything in my powers to make your life in this school as miserable as possible. And that's a promise.'

Ms Cerise stood up, picked up her marker pen and flounced over to the whiteboard. 'And if you are in any doubt why I'm doing this, then let me make it crystal clear.'

In big blue letters, she wrote on the whiteboard:

IT'S ALL <u>MILK'S</u> FAULT.

Everyone groaned, glaring at Milk. Their weekend was ruined.

'But Miss,' pleaded Milk, 'there's no need to punish everybody. That's not fair.'

But Ms Cerise was unmoved. In her sweetest, little-girliest voice she said, 'Seeing as I'm not totally heartless, you can all make a head start on your weekend reading. Open your books to page one. I'm sure you'll find Mr Thicke's explanation of logarithms absolutely fascinating.'

Milk's day only got worse.

After school she hurried back to Carp's Café hoping to find it open. But it was just as it had been that morning; blinds shut tight and no sign of Jarvis. Worse still, further along the promenade, she counted six coaches parked outside Café Smoooth. As the excited holidaymakers clambered out, the Mayor greeted each one with a friendly handshake, directing them towards the entrance of Café Smoooth.

So it was true. Even the Mayor was supporting the new café. It seemed like everyone had completely forgotten about Jarvis.

To top it all, it started to rain. Milk pulled her hood over her head and picked up her schoolbag. At first she couldn't figure out why it was much heavier than usual. But then she remembered she was carrying *Advanced Maths for Really Clever People*, and her mood sank even lower.

CHAPTER 11

PINK MASH AND PARMESAN

Grandad ambled into Milk's bedroom carrying the telephone.

'Morning Grandad,' yawned Milk. She turned and looked at the clock beside her bed. It was only just after six o'clock. 'You're up early.'

'I've been washing the car,' replied Grandad, sitting down on the end of her bed.

'But we haven't got a car.'

'Haven't we? That's a shame. I waxed it too.'

Milk liked talking to Grandad when she was half asleep. In those few drowsy moments she felt as comfortably befuddled as him.

'Maybe you were washing the cat,' she suggested.

Grandad thought for a moment. 'No, no, I'm pretty sure I wasn't washing the cat. Though that's a very good idea. Have you smelt his breath recently? It smells like blue cheese.'

Slowly, he got up and headed towards the door. 'I better go and wash the car then.'

Just as he was leaving, Milk noticed the telephone in his hand. 'Grandad, why have you got the telephone?'

'What telephone?' came the somewhat inevitable answer.

'The one in your hand.'

Grandad lifted his empty hand up to his face, examining it back and front for any trace of telephone.

'In your other hand,' smiled Milk. She sometimes wondered if Grandad really was that confused or if he just enjoyed playing tricks on her. Then again, he did seem genuinely surprised when he discovered the telephone in his other hand.

'Oh! Yes! There's a call for you,' he said, passing the phone to Milk.

'Who is it?' asked Milk, pressing the phone to her ear. 'Hello?'

'Milk? Milk? Can you hear me? It's me, Jarvis. You've got to come over quick. Something amazing has happened. You've got to see it. It's incredible!'

'Slow down,' urged Milk, sitting up in bed. 'What's happened?'

'I can't explain over the phone. Just come. As quick as you can.'

And with that he hung up.

Milk dressed as fast as she could and ran downstairs. In the kitchen sink, Grandad was already cleaning the cat's teeth with a paintbrush. 'She wouldn't let me brush her teeth unless I got in the sink with her,' explained Grandad, his long legs tucked up around his chin.

'She's a very lucky cat,' grinned Milk, going up on tiptoes to kiss his cheek. 'I'll see you later. I'll be at Carp's Café if you need me.'

As she hurried down the hill, Milk saw Mr Frat standing outside his house in his pyjamas. 'Do you know anything about this?' he growled, pointing at his car. It was sparkling clean and beautifully waxed. It looked as good as new. 'Who's been cleaning my car?'

'Maybe it was the fairies,' suggested Milk, skipping by.

'Rubbish,' he snorted, giving his bum a good scratch. 'And I heard you got your whole class in trouble too. Got them all extra homework. You should learn to keep your big mouth shut.'

Milk ignored him. In the upstairs window she spotted Frank and Fenella Frat, their sad faces steaming up the glass. Milk waved at them. Limply, they waved back before sliding back into the shadows.

Jarvis was waiting for her outside the café. His puffy cheeks were flushed pink with excitement. 'Quick, come inside.'

'What is it?' asked Milk. She could feel butterflies building up in her stomach. 'What's going on?'

He took her hand and led her inside the café, locking the door behind him.

Jarvis spoke quickly, the words tumbling out of his mouth like alphabet soup. 'When I came back from Café Smoooth the other night I felt terrible. I thought I was finished. I thought Carp's Café was finished. I stayed in bed all night and all day yesterday. I heard you calling for me, but I didn't want to see anyone. I'm sorry, Milk.'

'That's all right. I was worried, that's all. He's a horrible man, that Mr Blanket. Did you see his teeth?'

'Like a horse with a toffee,' said Jarvis with a smile. 'Anyhow, when I got up this morning, I thought I'd better clean up the kitchen. I hadn't been in there since we tried to make that porridge.'

Milk had never seen Jarvis like this before. He was jittery, pacing up and down.

'And that's when I found . . .'

'What?'

'In there,' he said, pointing towards the kitchen.

'What is it?'

At last, he stopped pacing. 'Take a look for yourself.'

Milk crossed the café and put her hand out to part the beaded curtains. She heard a faint scratching and scuttling sound, the same sound she had heard the previous morning. She turned and looked at Jarvis, who nodded, reassuring her it was safe to go in.

It was incredible!

Ants, thousands of them, swarmed all over the kitchen. They were everywhere, scurrying across the floor, over the surfaces, pouring in and out of the fridge and the cupboards.

'What are they doing?' gasped Milk, putting her hand over her mouth.

'They're building,' replied Jarvis, pointing towards the far side of the kitchen.

Rising from the worktop was a three-foot-high replica of the Eiffel Tower, made entirely out of Parmesan cheese. Ants hurried up and down the side of the tall yellow structure, squashing pieces of cheese into place, perfectly recreating the iron lattice tower in every detail. It was magnificent.

'It's amazing, isn't it?' said Jarvis, giving Milk a nudge.

Milk was dumbstruck. Eventually, she stuttered, 'How do they know what they're doing?'

'They're copying,' replied Jarvis, pointing to the picture of the Eiffel Tower on the wall. 'Every now and again you can see them looking at it.'

This was perhaps the craziest thing she had ever heard. Ants can't copy from pictures. She looked at Jarvis to see if he was pulling her leg.

'I'm not joking,' insisted Jarvis. 'See for yourself.'

Milk concentrated on a single ant climbing the Eiffel Tower. Sure enough, just as it reached the tallest point, the ant stopped and turned its head to look at the picture. After a moment's thought, the ant carefully positioned its tiny piece of Parmesan cheese, gently squashing it into place with its two back legs.

'You're right! I saw it looking!' squealed Milk, jumping up and down. 'It's amazing!'

'There's something else,' said Jarvis. 'Follow me.'

Ants scurried around their feet as they shuffled, inch by inch, towards the open fridge.

'Look at this,' whispered Jarvis, pushing opening the fridge door a little wider.

An orderly trail of ants led up to the third shelf of the fridge and into a large plastic bowl. The trail re-emerged on the other side of the bowl with each ant carrying a tiny piece of pink, fluffy stuff squidged on its back.

'What is it?' asked Milk, leaning into the fridge.

'Mashed potato,' replied Jarvis. 'I made it the other day to go with the eel and spicy pineapple pie.'

'But why is it pink?'

'That's what I wondered. But then I saw this.'

He pointed at a little bottle that lay on its side next to the bowl of mashed potato. The lid was off and the bottle was empty.

'It's red food colouring,' explained Jarvis. 'The ants must have found it in the cupboard, carried it across the kitchen, unscrewed the lid and poured it into the mashed potato.'

Milk started to giggle. It was all so fantastically strange.

'But why do they want pink mashed potato?' she asked.

'You'll see,' grinned Jarvis.

They followed the trail of ants out of the bowl, back down to the floor and round behind the fridge door. That's when she saw it: a pink mashed potato replica of the Taj Mahal. It was as tall as Milk's waist and as wide as Jarvis's tummy and decorated with hundreds of tiny pieces of orange and lemon peel. It was just as it was in Jarvis's picture.

'Jarvis,' gasped Milk. 'It's beautiful.'

'They're building the pyramids here,' said Jarvis, pointing at a rising pile of sugar cubes. 'And if you were here earlier you would have seen the Leaning Tower of Pisa made out of butter.' He pointed at a pool of yellow liquid dripping off the surface next to the microwave. 'I guess it must have melted.'

'But they're ants. How are they doing it?'

In a way, Milk already knew the answer. But it seemed so ridiculous, so impossible, that she daren't say it out loud.

'I think the ants must have eaten the Porridge of Knowledge and it's made them . . . clever.'

'Super clever,' added Milk.

'I can't think of any other explanation.'

'Nor me.'

They stood in silence for a long while, gazing at the mini-wonders of the world all around them.

Suddenly, Milk announced, 'We have to be sure.'

'You're right,' agreed Jarvis, nodding slowly. 'What do you mean?'

'We have to be sure if it's the porridge doing this or if it's just one of those, you know, freaks of nature.'

'Like you see on TV?' asked Jarvis. '*Freaks of the Animal Kingdom*. I love that programme.'

'Exactly.'

'I saw one episode where there was this farm in America that was next to a school playground and all the cows had taught themselves to play kiss chase just by watching the children at playtime. It was amazing, seeing cows kissing.'

Milk looked over at her friend, her eyes shining with admiration. 'Jarvis, you're brilliant.'

'I am?'

'You are,' she insisted, shuffling towards the cooker. 'Here, give me a hand with the pot.'

CHAPTER 12

TOY TOWN

They carried the porridge pot out of the kitchen and into the café. It was still half full and thankfully, it didn't smell nearly as bad as before. In fact, it smelt almost sweet . . . well, *mouldysweet*; a bit like a bar of chocolate that's been lying around in the back of a cupboard for twenty years.

Jarvis began hacking at the porridge with a knife, breaking the dried-up mixture into chunks. With a spoon, Milk scooped out the chunks and put them into Tupperware boxes, squashing a lid onto each one. When they were done, they had eight boxes, full to the brim.

'What else do we need?' asked Jarvis.

'Nothing,' replied Milk, tucking one of the Tupperwares under her arm. 'Let's go.'

It was that most rare thing in Slopp-on-Sea – a beautiful day. The morning sun climbed proudly into the sky, banishing any pesky clouds. Milk and Jarvis strode through the village and up a muddy track that led to the hills beyond. Hedgerows heavy with blackberries towered above them and all around, yellow splashes of dandelion littered the banks. The track narrowed. Ivy grew up and over them, turning the track into a tunnel.

'Not far now,' puffed Milk, her shoes heavy with mud.

She turned to see Jarvis struggling some way back. It was heavy going for the heavy man. As she waited for him to catch up, she tried to remember the first time they had ever met. But it wasn't possible; Jarvis had always just been *there*. She remembered sitting on her grandmother's lap, watching Jarvis and Grandad playing chess in the café. Neither of them knew the rules, they just took turns moving the pieces around the chess board, making up far-fetched stories about the king's double chin or the bishop's underpants or a fearsome tribe of cannibal pawns. When Grandma died, Jarvis filled his café with flowers and for months after told wonderful stories about her to anyone who cared to listen.

'Hurry up, slow coach,' teased Milk, as Jarvis drew level.

'Are we there yet?' asked Jarvis. He was panting like an old dog and his trousers were totally splattered with mud.

'Just a bit further. Here, let me help.' And she went behind him and pushed against his back. Like a top-heavy pantomime horse they squilched-squelched up the track. At last, the slope began to level off. Dappled sun streaked through the ivy canopy, until suddenly they spilt out into open countryside.

Days like this, so few and far between, made Milk realise how lucky she was to live in Slopp-on-Sea. In front of her sprawled a vast panorama of green fields with small patches of woodland dotted about in the distance. A field full of black-and-white cows looked lazily over in their direction. Seeing nothing of interest, they went back to their grazing, cowbells gently clanging as they moooved.

Milk turned to face the sea, which curved away over the horizon. It was easy to see why people once believed that this was the edge of the world, where the sea fell away into a giant waterfall. And if that wasn't enough to keep fishermen close to shore, there were always the legends of diabolical sea monsters.

From this height Slopp-on-Sea resembled little more than a toy town, with miniature people going in and out of toy houses, and toy coaches vrooming along the curved promenade towards the toy pier, on the end of which stood a broken, wind-up Ferris wheel.

Suddenly, Jarvis boomed out at the toy town beneath them, 'I've got ants in my kitchen!' He turned and grinned at Milk like a cheeky schoolboy.

Milk giggled and followed suit, yelling, 'Ms Cerise is an old fart!'

Jarvis's turn. 'Café Smoooth is on fire!'

Then Milk. 'Greasy Reecey Blanket!'

And so on and so on until their throats were hoarse and their giggles dissolved into the morning sky.

CHAPTER 13

THE COWS

Milk stood on the wooden fence waving a handful of freshly picked grass.

'Come on, cow. Come to Milky.'

'Here, cowey, cowey, cowey,' sweet-talked Jarvis.

But the cows ignored them.

'Right,' announced Milk impatiently. 'I'm going in.'

She tucked the Tupperware full of porridge under her arm and clambered over the fence.

'Are you sure it's safe?' asked Jarvis.

'They're only cows. I'll be fine.'

That said, her heart started beating just a little quicker as she approached the cows. They might look gentle, she told herself, but they're certainly big and heavy. It wouldn't take much on their part to squash a ten-year-old girl.

One by one, the cows, all eight of them, stopped grazing and stared at Milk.

'Don't worry, Milk,' she muttered under her breath,

'that's what cows do. They stare.'

She took a couple of steps closer, then very slowly peeled off the lid of the Tupperware. One cow flicked its ear, another swished its tail. Milk took out a lump of porridge and in a gentle underarm throw, tossed it in the direction of the nearest cow.

'Go on, moo-cow. Eat it.'

But the cow didn't budge.

She threw another piece. This time the porridge landed right in between two cows.

Nothing. Just more stares. She took a step forward and tried a third and a fourth time, but still the cows took no notice.

One lump left. Now she was getting irritated. This wasn't part of the plan. On the way up here, she'd imagined the whole herd happily trotting over to the fence and gratefully nibbling porridge out of her hand. Surely cows got bored with grass day in, day out.

'Come on, you stupid cows,' she yelled. 'Eat the porridge!'

Overarm, she hurled the final lump. She didn't mean it to hit a cow smack on the end of its nose . . . but it did.

In a chorus of moos, they charged.

'RUN!' howled Jarvis.

Milk dropped the Tupperware and sprinted. Dried flecks of mud flew off her shoes as she sprinted back towards the fence. She felt sure she could outrun them: after all, cows can't gallop. Can they?

'Keep going,' bellowed Jarvis. 'You're nearly there.'

Milk looked behind her. Sure enough, the cows were falling behind. It was going to be OK. She was going to make it . . .

Just then, her foot splat-landed in an enormous, sloppy cowpat. Milk skidded up into the air, somersaulting twice before slamming onto the grass. Semi-dazed, she raised her head to see eight mad cows rampaging towards her. She tried to get up but her arms and legs had turned to jelly. She could see the whites of the cows' eyes, saliva slobbering out of their mouths, ears pricked, udders swinging, cowbells clanging.

Then something happened that she never expected to see.

Out of nowhere, Jarvis bounded over Milk, landing between her and the cows. Ripping off his shirt, he slapped his

enormous belly and roared, 'MOOOARRRGGGHHHH!!!'

It was a wild, bullish display. The cows stopped dead in their tracks. For a moment, neither cows nor Jarvis moved, each eyeballing the other. And then, with a sharp jerk of their heads, the cows turned back into the field and continued their grazing as if nothing had happened.

From behind the safety of the fence, Milk and Jarvis waited patiently as the cows circled the lumps of porridge.

'They're getting closer,' said Milk, scraping cowpat off her shoe with a stick.

At last, one of the cows ambled over to a lump of porridge and gave it a sniff.

Milk crossed her fingers for luck. 'Please, Mr Cow. Eat it.'

'It's Mrs Cow,' corrected Jarvis, trying to squeeze his belly back into his buttonless shirt.

And then a cow – let's call her Daisy – ate the porridge. She chewed and chewed and chewed, her jaws moving from side to side. Not long after, a second cow found another lump of porridge and gobbled it up. Then a third, and a fourth, until all five lumps had been eaten.

'How will we know if it's working?' asked Jarvis.

'I don't know,' replied Milk, lying down in the grass. 'We'll just have to wait.'

She plucked a single blade of grass and put it in her mouth, twizzling it back and forth through a gap in her teeth. Overhead, a solitary cloud drifted through the sky, languidly shape-shifting from a one-legged giraffe into a dog cocking its leg. Milk closed her eyes. In the distance she could hear the Slopp church bells chiming. She used to come up here as a little girl, particularly in winter when it had been snowing. Grandad had built a toboggan entirely out of driftwood he'd found on the beach. Then, for some peculiar reason, he'd covered it completely in tin foil. The effect was remarkable, like a silver chariot fit for a fairy tale. And the best thing was that it was big enough for two.

'I'm not going to let you have all the fun by yourself,' puffed Grandad as he hauled the toboggan up the snowy hill. At the top, Grandad sat at the back with Milk tucked in between his outstretched legs. In those days, the slope seemed incredibly steep and Milk would half-cover her eyes with her gloved hands.

'Ready?' asked Grandad.

Milk nodded.

'Are you sure? It's going to be fast. Our Silver Snow Machine can reach speeds of one hundred miles an hour.'

Milk gulped, but nodded again. With Grandad she felt ready for anything.

'Well, let's goooooo!'

And off they went, careering down the hill, screeching like teenagers at a funfair. The silver toboggan picked up speed, scattering surprised squirrels as it skidded effortlessly over the snow. It felt like at any minute they could take off and fly all the way down into Slopp toy town, in time for hot chocolate at Carp's Café . . .

* * *

'Milk! Wake up. Look!' Jarvis was on his feet, pointing towards the cows. 'Something's happening.'

Milk opened her eyes and sat up. Of the eight cows, five were shuddering, shaking like leaves.

And then the strangeness began.

One by one, the five cows sat down on their rumps, in a circle, facing each other, with their hind legs sticking out in front of them.

'What are they doing?' asked Milk, rubbing her eyes.

For a moment the cows just sat there, as if they were about to discuss important cow business (udder hygiene, cowpat disposal, etc.) – until, following Daisy's lead, they began twitching their heads, just enough to ring the cowbells tied around their necks.

Straight away, Jarvis realised what the cows were doing. 'They're copying the church bells!' he said excitedly. 'They must hear them all the time. Listen.'

He was right. The cows were ringing their cowbells perfectly in time with the sound of the Slopp church bells.

'It's the porridge,' squealed Milk, clapping her hands together. 'It must be! It's working!'

But that wasn't the last of it. As the day drifted by, Jarvis and Milk watched, enthralled, as the cows performed a series of remarkable feats. They played hoofball, kicking the Tupperware container up and down the field, using freshly made cowpats as goalposts. They dabbled in acrobatics, including a most impressive five-cow pyramid, and to top it all, they drew caveman-style mud paintings on the side of their water trough, using their tails as paintbrushes.

And then it was over. With a tiny shudder, they became normal, everyday drooling cows once again. The effect of the porridge had worn off.

Flushed with success (and the late-evening sun), Milk and Jarvis headed home.

CHAPTER 14

JITTERBUGS

Milk was the first to notice them: unwelcome shadows flickering inside Carp's Café.

'There's someone in there,' she said, in a nervous whisper.

'Maybe it's the ants,' suggested Jarvis.

'It doesn't look like it. That's something much bigger.'

They moved a little closer towards the café. It was getting dark but the street lights along the promenade had yet to come on.

Jarvis's imagination shifted up a gear. 'What if the ants have grown and changed into *super*-ants?'

The giant shadows twirled and twisted, pulsating against the walls of the café.

'Weapons,' declared Milk suddenly. 'We need weapons.'

They looked around them, but a seaside promenade makes for a disappointing armoury. All they could find were ice-lolly sticks and half a saveloy; hardly the type of weapons to strike fear into giant ants.

Milk threw the half-saveloy back into the gutter. 'Wait there a minute,' she said and hurried across the road. She ducked through a hole in the wire fence and disappeared into the darkness of the abandoned, weed-filled public tennis court. Moments later she reappeared clutching two terrifying weapons: a broken tennis racket missing all its strings and a handful of tall stinging nettles that she clutched in the sleeve of her jacket.

'You take the racket,' she said, handing it to him, 'and I'll sting them.'

Suitably armed, they tiptoed towards the café. Fog had steamed up the windows. They couldn't see in.

'I can hear music,' squeaked Jarvis in the tiniest of voices. 'What's going on?'

'There's only one way to find out.' Milk put her hand up against the café door, preparing to charge. 'Are you ready?'

Jarvis nodded.

'On three. One, two . . .'

'Wait, wait, wait,' whispered Jarvis. 'Who's going in first?'

'Well, who's got the best weapon?'

They quickly agreed that being stung by nettles was worse than a whack over the head with a tennis racket.

Milk stepped in front of Jarvis. 'Ready, steady, GO!' And with a bloodcurdling yell she flung open the door.

There wasn't a giant ant in sight. On every available surface were dozens of candles gently flickering out a soft, warm light. All the tables and chairs had been moved to the sides and there, in the middle, were Alfred and Irene, jitterbugging to an old tune blaring out from the café radio.

'There you are!' beamed Alfred, swinging Irene through his legs and back out again. 'We wondered where you got to.'

'Hope you don't mind, we moved the furniture,' squealed Irene, flapping her skirt from side to side.

'We tried dancing between the tables, but there simply wasn't enough room. We'll put it all back later, won't we, sweetheart?' And he pulled Irene towards him and planted a giant smacker on her lips.

Milk and Jarvis were rooted to the spot. Not in their wildest dreams had they ever expected to see Alfred and Irene – the argumentative, semi-crippled geriatrics – dancing riotously by candlelight in the café. This was far stranger than giant ants.

'Have you been playing tennis?' asked Irene, jiving past Jarvis's upheld racket.

Jarvis shook his head. He was speechless.

'We should play some time. I love tennis!' And she snatched the racket out of his hand and began strumming it like a guitar.

'Where are your walking sticks?' asked Milk.

'Whaddaya need *walking* sticks for when you're *dancing*?!' yelped Alfred.

'And you're not arguing,' Jarvis said. 'You always argue.'

Just then, with a blast of bass saxophone, the song finished. Alfred and Irene collapsed on the floor in a fit of giggles.

Grinning, Irene looked up at Jarvis. 'The door was open,' she puffed, catching her breath. 'We helped ourselves to tea and flapjacks. They were delicious, by the way. I hope you don't mind.'

'What flapjacks? I haven't made flapjacks,' said Jarvis.

'The ones on the counter. In the Tupperware.'

The penny dropped. Jarvis and Milk looked down at the happy couple frolicking on the floor.

'They've had the porridge!' whispered Jarvis.

'I know,' Milk whispered back.

'But I thought it was meant to make you clever. Not . . . crazy.'

'Me too. It must work in different ways.'

Alfred got to his feet, pulling up Irene after him. 'Come on, darling. We've got work to do.'

Alfred and Irene began lifting tables and chairs, putting everything back in its right place. Milk and Jarvis tried to help, but the old couple wouldn't hear of it. 'Tut tut. This is our mess. You two sit yourselves down. You must be tired after your tennis.'

And so Milk and Jarvis sat down and watched incredulously as they tidied everything up.

'Time for us old folk to go home,' said Irene, tucking their four walking sticks under her arm.

Alfred thrust a £20 note into Jarvis's hand. With a twinkle in his eye, he said, 'Keep the change. We've got to make sure a fine café like this never closes. You won't find us at that rotten Café Smoooth.'

And with that, he offered his arm to Irene and together they skipped out of the door like a pair of spring rabbits.

For a long time Jarvis and Milk sat on their chairs without saying a word. They could hardly believe what they had just witnessed.

'It's been quite a day,' said Milk eventually, picking up the large plastic tomato in front of her and squeezing a tiny dollop of ketchup onto the back of her hand.

Jarvis got up and poked his head through the beaded curtains. 'The ants have all gone.'

Milk licked the ketchup off her hand. Then she said what they were both thinking. 'We've got to try the porridge.'

'We must,' agreed Jarvis.

'When?'

'How about tomorrow? It's Sunday. The café's closed and you've got no school.'

'Tomorrow then,' said Milk, with a smile.

'Tomorrow,' repeated Jarvis.

CHAPTER 15

PORRIDGE ON THE BRAIN

Sleep was out of the question.

Every time Milk closed her eyes she saw cows scaling the Eiffel Tower or ants jitterbugging or Alfred and Irene playing tennis wearing cowbells. It was all too much. She had porridge on the brain.

Outside, the rain clattered against her bedroom window. *At least that's normal*, she thought. *As long as it's raining, not everything is topsy-turvy.* She remembered when she was little and couldn't sleep, Grandma would sit at the end of her bed and sing to her, over and over . . .

'You can set your clock
By the rain in Slopp.
Tick tock, tick tock
By the rain in Slopp.'

And if that didn't work and Milk *still* couldn't sleep then

Grandad would come upstairs and tell her the story of how she came to live with them.

He always began the same way. '*Once upon a time there was an old man and an old woman who lived by the sea . . .*'

And with those familiar words Milk would close her eyes and let the first flush of sleep wash over her.

'*And one day, a baby came into their lives. She had two teeny-weeny arms and two teeny-weeny legs and nine teeny-weeny toes . . .*'

'Ten toes,' giggled Milk groggily. 'I've got ten toes.'

'*And the little baby was the most beautiful thing they had ever seen and the old man and the old woman were the happiest people in the whole wide world . . .*'

And the sound of the rain mingled with Grandad's mellifluous voice until Milk sank into a deep, deep sleep.

Now she was ten, she was, of course, far too old for such things, though some small part of her still ached for Grandad to tell her the story one more time.

Milk switched on the light and checked the clock. It was only two thirty-three; ages before daylight. On the floor she saw her copy of *Advanced Maths for Really Clever People* poking out of the top of her schoolbag. The test was tomorrow and she hadn't done a thing about it. She imagined explaining to Ms Cerise why she hadn't done her reading, telling her the truth about the porridge and the ants and the cows. Of course, Ms Cerise wouldn't believe her. Who would? She'd be better off telling Ms Cerise that evil mushrooms from outer space had abducted her and cruelly experimented with her brain. Somehow, that would be more believable.

Without getting out of bed, Milk stretched to the floor and picked up *Advanced Maths for Really Clever People*, opening it at chapter one.

Numbers and symbols and fiendish equations lurked on every page and however hard she tried, none of it seemed to make any sense whatsoever. For example:

Farmer x has 243 chickens. Farmer y has 24% fewer chickens than Farmer x. Each chicken lays 4 eggs a day. Using the equation x + y = scrambled eggs, work out which farmer has the longest beard.

What?! It was too difficult. All she could see was a hotchpotch of numbers, jumbling about on the page. Her eyes went fuzzy. A disobedient '4' began sliding down the page in looping spirals. She blinked. *Concentrate, Milk, you can do this. Farmer x has 243 chickens . . .* But it was no good. The disobedient '4' began skating arm in arm with the '*x*' and the '%' pirouetted down the side of the page. Milk gave up. *Let them dance*, she thought and with blank, staring eyes she watched the numbers swirl across the page in a curious mathematical waltz.

Eventually, Milk tossed the book back onto the floor and re-checked the clock. Two forty-one. Only eight minutes had passed. Why was it that time moved so slowly in the middle of the night? She looked around, searching for something to do. There were old comics and magazines piled up in the corner of the room, and on the shelf was her collection of beach-pebbles-that-resembled-film-stars. Clothes were

strewn all over the floor and on the table there were three half-eaten apple cores all turning various shades of brown. It was fair to say she was not a tidy girl. It crossed her mind to tidy up, but even the thought of it made her brain ache.

There was nothing else for it. She decided to go for a walk. She didn't care that it was still raining; the night air might clear her head.

She dressed and went downstairs, almost treading on Grandad. He was sleeping on the rug at the bottom of the stairs. The cat stretched out along one of his legs, like some great furry sock.

As Milk crept past him, Grandad opened one eye. 'Where are you going?' he asked.

'Nowhere,' replied Milk. 'I'm going for a walk. I can't sleep.'

One-eyed Grandad looked at her for the longest time, as if he was trying to remember something. Eventually he smiled and said, 'Once upon a time there was an old man and an old woman who lived by the sea . . .' before closing his eye and drifting back to sleep.

Milk wrapped the rug around him, found her umbrella, the see-through one with frogs on, and went outside.

It was chucking it down – bucketing! – rat-rat-rattling rain beating against her umbrella like marbles in a tin can. At the bottom of the hill, Milk crossed the road onto the promenade. She looked out to the sea, which churned and groaned and spat out great waves onto the pebbled beach. Curiously for this time of night, there were lights coming from the direction of the pier. Milk stopped at her telescope, found her 20p stuck with old chewing gum and put the coin in the slot. It was hard to see anything through the rain. She could just make out the shape of a vehicle reversing onto the pier before the telescope clicked shut. Probably just a late delivery for Café Smoooth, she told herself. She pulled her froggy umbrella right down to her shoulders and marched on through the driving rain.

Sleep was out of the question.

Every time Jarvis closed his eyes he saw cows sliding down the pyramids of Giza or ants ringing church bells or Alfred and Irene play-fighting with pink mashed potato. He, too, had porridge on the brain.

Jarvis switched on the light and checked the clock. It was only two thirty-three; ages before daylight. He sat up in his bed and looked around the room, searching for something to do. It was the same room he had slept in all his life. Very little had changed since he was a boy. The toys he used to play with were still in the trunk under the window, and apart from a few new cookery books the shelves were full of the same adventure stories that he used to read over and over. Hovering above his bed were three model birds, suspended from the ceiling with fishing wire: a blackbird, a seagull and a pigeon, all made with real feathers glued onto tightly scrunched-up balls of toilet paper. At the time, nine-year-old Jarvis was extremely proud of his creations, but now, thirty-three years later, he had to admit they were looking very ropey; the blackbird's marble eyes had fallen out and the seagull had lost so many feathers it looked like a shrivelled sausage with wings.

Jarvis re-checked the clock. Two forty-one. Only eight minutes had passed. Why was it that time moved so slowly in the middle of the night? With a noisy yawn and a bone clicking stretch, he clambered out of bed and crossed the room, taking a seat on his old toy trunk. On the windowsill he saw his donkey sweet dispenser; pull its plastic tail and with a noise that sounds nothing like a donkey, a boiled sweet pops out of its gaping mouth. Jarvis pulled the tail three times and put all three sweets in his mouth at the same time. His record was fourteen, but at this time of night he wasn't in the mood for record breaking. For a while he just sat and sucked, boiled sweets clacking against his teeth, daydreaming in the middle of the night. Eventually, as the last slither of sweet trickled down his throat, he reached up and pulled open the curtains. Outside, the rain was hammering against his window and the sea roared furiously, like a wounded lion. Further down the promenade he could just make out the shape of a vehicle reversing onto the pier. Probably just a late delivery for Café Smoooth, he told himself. It was then he saw a lone figure wandering along the promenade, huddled under an umbrella. Who on earth would be out on a night like this? As the figure drew closer, he recognised the little green frogs that decorated the umbrella.

'Milk!' he exclaimed, leaping to his feet.

Quickly, he pulled on his dressing gown and slippers and hurried downstairs.

CHAPTER 16

ALNITAK, ALNILAM AND MINTAKA

Jarvis came through from the kitchen carrying his two best plates.

'Which one would you like?' he asked, holding them up for Milk's inspection.

On one plate was a goofy, gooey photo of a blobby royal baby. On the other was a painting of three overweight children sitting on a donkey at the beach. Milk chose the first plate; she liked the way the baby's puffy eyes seemed to follow her wherever she moved.

Ceremoniously, Jarvis laid the plates onto the table. Then, from his dressing gown pocket he took out two silver teaspoons. With the end of his dressing gown cord he gave them a thorough polish before putting them next to the plates. Every action was carried out with purpose and precision, as if to say, *If we're going to do this, then we're going to do it properly.*

Milk felt it too. 'Napkins?' she suggested.

'Good idea,' replied Jarvis.

He opened a drawer and took out two napkins. *Cloth* napkins, no less; no paper rubbish on an occasion such as this.

Like the queen's butler, Jarvis fetched one of the Tupperware boxes and laid it on the café table. As he removed the lid, a familiar waft of mouldysweetness filled the air – it was definitely improving with age, thought Milk. Then he sliced two portions of porridge and put one on each plate.

It was time to eat.

Jarvis sat down opposite Milk. His hands were trembling – just a little. Nerves began to get the better of Milk too. She started giggling; her lump of porridge sat directly over the royal baby's nose, making him look even blobbier than before.

'You first,' said Jarvis.

'No. You first,' replied Milk, trying to wipe the smile off her face.

'All right then.' He picked up his lump of porridge and shoved the whole thing into his mouth.

'Your turn,' he said in between chews.

This is it. There's no going back.

Milk screwed up her eyes and chucked the porridge into her mouth.

Surprisingly, it didn't taste too bad. Not super-sweet, but certainly not disgusting. Though the outside was hard, the inside was quite soft and gooey, much like a meringue. Mechanically, her teeth crunched and chewed and minced until at last she was able to swallow.

She opened her eyes. The blobby baby looked back at her.

'Now what?' asked Jarvis, wiping the corners of his mouth with the napkin. They had both forgotten to use their teaspoons.

Milk looked around the café to see if anything was different, but everything seemed just the same. She didn't really know what to do with herself.

'Shall we put some music on?' she suggested.

'Good idea.' Jarvis got up and switched on the radio. Grandiose opera music filled the café. Normally she would have asked Jarvis to change the radio station – opera was not her favourite – but now, the melodramatic warbling seemed just right for the occasion.

She got up and looked out of the café window. It was still the middle of the night. The rain had stopped and some of the clouds had parted to reveal a handful of waterlogged stars. And then . . .

Milk shuddered.

It was a tiny shudder, almost unnoticeable.

That's all it was.

The Porridge of Knowledge had begun its work.

Milk squinted up at the night sky. Without thinking, she said, 'Alnitak, Alnilam and Mintaka.'

'What did you say?' asked Jarvis.

Milk pointed. 'Those three stars. That's their names: Alnitak, Alnilam and Mintaka. Together they're known as Orion's Belt.'

'How do you know?' quizzed Jarvis.

'I just know,' replied Milk, with absolute confidence.

And then Jarvis shuddered.

He stood next to Milk. 'And there's Betelgeuse and Rigel. They're the two brightest stars in the Orion constellation.'

'Exactly,' replied Milk.

They both stopped and looked at each other. Neither of them knew a thing about astronomy, yet here they were rattling off the names of the stars like experts.

'Do you feel at all . . . different?' asked Milk.

'I don't think so. I feel the same, I think.'

'Are we clever?'

'I don't feel particularly clever,' replied Jarvis.

'Maybe we're the cleverest people in the world,' declared Milk. Her eyes were twinkling like Betelgeuse. 'We need to test it.'

'How? What do clever people do?'

'I don't know,' replied Milk, looking around the café for something to do. 'What about a game?'

'How about hide and seek?'

'No!' giggled Milk. 'A clever game.'

'I know!' announced Jarvis, throwing his hands in the air. 'Chess! It's the cleverest game of all. I've got a set upstairs.'

'But I don't know how to play chess,' said Milk.

'Nor do I.' And with that Jarvis scurried upstairs to get his chess set.

Chess is a notoriously difficult game that can take years to master. Each piece moves in a number of different ways and with each move there are hundreds of possibilities and consequences. And yet, within minutes both Milk and Jarvis were playing with such speed and brilliance it would make

a chess grandmaster blush. Their porridge-fuelled brains were like computers that fizzed and crackled and told them exactly what move to make next. The brainiest game in the world was as easy to them as snakes and ladders.

They played for a long time; it must have been hours, because the next time Milk looked up, morning sun was streaming through the café window. Her body felt stiff and her stomach rumbled furiously, demanding attention.

'I'm hungry,' she announced.

'Me too,' replied Jarvis, getting to his feet. 'Jam sandwich?'

'Perfect.'

As Jarvis plodded into the kitchen, Milk pushed back her chair, stretched out her arms and let out a yawn so big it could have come from a person twice her size. Giant Milk. She ambled over to the café window and looked out onto the empty promenade. What a night it had been. Beyond her wildest expectations. *And this*, she said to herself, *is just the beginning.*

Just then, a strange sound came from the kitchen – like a smash and a splodge at the same time.

'Jarvis? Are you OK?'

There was no answer. Milk hurried through the beaded curtain into the kitchen.

In front of the open fridge stood Jarvis, motionless, holding a lid. At his feet was a smashed jar of strawberry jam.

'What happened?' asked Milk.

Jarvis looked up at her. His face was as white as a sheet. 'The jam. I . . .'

'You dropped it. It doesn't matter. We can have something else in our sandwiches.'

'You don't understand,' insisted Jarvis. Tears began welling up in his eyes. 'Milk. The strawberry jam. I *smelt* it. I actually smelt it.'

Since the day he shoved all those peanuts up his nostrils in a playground dare, Jarvis hadn't smelt a thing.

'I took the lid off the jam and there was this incredible smell of strawberries.'

'Can you smell it now?' asked Milk. 'Try again.'

Jarvis brought the lid to his nose and inhaled deeply. His whole body seemed to inflate with pleasure.

'It smells . . . beautiful!'

'It's the porridge,' cried Milk happily. 'You can smell because of the Porridge of Knowledge.'

But Jarvis wasn't listening. Already he was over by the spice rack, filling his nostrils. Cardamom, cinnamon, cumin, paprika, coriander; each new smell sent him into spirals of joy.

And then a thought popped into his aroma-addled brain. A thought so ludicrous, so wonderful, he hardly dared say it.

'Milk. If I can smell, do you think I might be able to . . . taste?'

In all his life, Jarvis had never tasted a thing. Nothing. Not a banana, not vanilla ice cream, not a sausage. 'If I *can* taste,' he added, 'what should I try first?'

What do you give someone who has never tasted anything? Cheese? Bovril? Honey? Marmalade? Mashed potato? What about cabbage or Brussels sprouts?

It had to be something special. Very special indeed. Milk racked her brain.

And then she got it. Of course! Her favourite thing. Something she would quite happily have every day, with every meal.

Ketchup.

'Wait there,' she said and hurried back into the café. There were large plastic tomatoes on every table, each one full of delicious, mouth-watering ketchup. Milk grabbed one from the nearest table and just to be sure, squirted a dollop straight into her gob. It tasted perfect; sharp and sweet. She couldn't think of a better food for Jarvis's first ever taste.

In the kitchen, she squeezed a tiny blob onto a teaspoon and handed it to Jarvis.

'I hope you like it.'

'I hope I can taste it,' replied Jarvis. His hand was shaking.

'Go on then,' encouraged Milk.

And he did.

Imagine, if you will, coming out of a cave and seeing the sun shining in the sky for the first time. That's just how Jarvis felt as the tomato ketchup swilled around his mouth. His whole body shivered and his hair stood on end. If this was a cartoon, steam would have gushed out of his ears and his nose would have trumpeted a delirious fanfare.

It was all too much. Like a baby giraffe, his legs gave way and he collapsed to the floor.

'Jarvis!' cried Milk. 'What's happened? Are you OK?'

He lay there, totally still. Milk knelt over him. Honestly, she thought he was a goner.

At last, he opened his eyes. 'MORE!' he roared. 'GIVE ME SOME MORE!'

Milk obliged. She squirted ketchup directly from the plastic tomato into his mouth. Jarvis's eyes rolled into the back of his head. He was in heaven.

'That's magnificent,' he purred. 'What's next?'

It could only be one thing. Chocolate. Milk scurried around the kitchen looking for something chocolatey. At the back of a cupboard she found a packet of cocoa powder, the type you use to make hot chocolate. She flicked open the packet and held it out to him.

'I can't move. Pour it in!' insisted Jarvis.

She didn't bother with a spoon. Instead, she held the packet over his face and tilted. An avalanche of cocoa powder exploded onto his face.

'Sorry!' giggled Milk. 'I didn't think it would come out so fast.'

Jarvis didn't mind one little bit. He sprung to his feet and did what would be forever remembered as his Chocolate Dance.

There was no stopping him now. Jarvis skipped over to the fridge and began stuffing everything into his mouth: butter, cheese, mustard, ham, greeting each new flavour with ecstatic *ooohs* and *ahhhs*.

Milk perched herself on the counter by the sink and watched his wild feeding frenzy. It went on and on: cucumber, blancmange, yogurt, salami, bananas, squirty cream; all met with hoots of delight. In fact, the only thing he didn't like was cabbage. But then again, nobody likes cabbage, do they?

After he had tried everything in the fridge two or three times, Jarvis slumped to the floor, happily rubbing his swollen belly.

'How are you feeling, greedy guts?' asked Milk, as she slipped down off the counter.

'Wonderful,' he replied. His eyes were glistening with joy. 'Do you know what this means, Milk? If I can taste and smell, I might become a better chef. And if I become a better chef, then maybe people will start coming back to Carp's Café. All I need is a little bit of porridge every day . . .'

'And I could be brilliant at school,' added Milk, considering the possibilities. 'Ms Cerise wouldn't know what was going on.' The thought tickled her no end. In fact, it gave her a brilliant idea. 'Jarvis, can you help me make two normal flapjacks and some chocolate topping?'

'Of course,' he said, as he picked up the can of squirty cream off the floor. 'Just as soon as I've tried this.'

'But you've already tried that. I saw you.'

'Did I? Oh well. One more try can't hurt.' And he flipped off the lid and aimed the nozzle into his mouth.

CHAPTER 17

MERMAID'S FLUNGE

Curiously, when Milk opened her eyes it was still dark; not pitch black, but a strange, murky, yellowy darkness. She had no idea where she was. Whatever she was lying on was cold and hard – certainly not her own bed – and her whole body ached from top to toe. Still half asleep, she reached up and felt something damp draped across her face, like the tentacle of a baby octopus. Slowly, tentatively, she peeled it away, squinting as her eyes grew accustomed to the daylight, until at last she realised she was holding nothing more sinister than a soggy banana skin.

With great effort she pushed herself up. A startled cockroach shot out from an empty yoghurt pot and scuttled off under the fridge. She saw Jarvis, lying on his side, with his head resting on the bottom shelf of the fridge. A dollop of blancmange clung to his cheek and he was snoring peacefully. Scattered around him was the debris of his feeding frenzy: broken eggs, spilt milk, spinach leaves, olive stones, half-eaten carrots, splashes of mayonnaise; he had really gone to town.

Milk looked at her watch. It was eight o'clock. In the morning! *Monday* morning! She'd slept all night on the kitchen floor. School started in an hour!

She leapt up, scattering a pile of empty crisp packets. If she hurried she could run home, wash, change into her school uniform and be at school just on time. She darted out of the kitchen and through the café. As she flung open the café door, she suddenly remembered the Tupperware she had carefully prepared the previous evening. She rushed back across the café, retrieved the Tupperware from the counter by the till and ran outside.

It was quite a surprise to see so many people on the promenade – there were never this many people out on a Monday morning – all of them looking out towards the sea. Perhaps a dolphin was swimming close to the shore or a pod of seals was frolicking in the surf. It sometimes happened and when it did, it would cause considerable excitement, especially amongst the holidaymakers. The further she went, the crowds got bigger, and at one point, there were people standing on the wall to get a better view. At last, curiosity got the better of her and she crossed the road to see what all the fuss was about.

She pushed through the crowd of people and peered over the promenade wall. What she saw took her breath away.

Dead fish, thousands of them, scattered across the beach as far as the eye could see. In some places the pebbles were completely obscured by silvery carcasses glistening in the morning light. There were bigger fish too. Some way along Milk thought she could see a dolphin washed up onto the beach. More fish bobbed pathetically in the water, drifting back and forth in the waves.

Already rumours were flying through the crowd.

'Maybe an oil tanker ran aground and spilt its cargo,' said one.

'No, they're diseased,' said another.

A third voice caught Milk's attention.

'I can't see what all the fuss is about. They're only fish, for goodness' sake.'

Milk turned to see she was standing next to Malcolm Blanket, the odious owner of Café Smoooth. He wore a suit that was at least three sizes too big, with pointy shoulder pads that jutted right out.

'In my mind,' he continued, 'fish are only good for one thing and that's caviar. Makes me hungry just looking at this lot.' That strange gargling noise came from the back of his throat, like a weasel being strangled. He was trying to laugh.

Next to him stood Mrs Blanket, holding her nose. 'And what a terrible smell. I do hope someone cleans it up soon or all my clothes will stink.' With her free hand she pulled a bottle of expensive-looking perfume out of her handbag and sprayed it all around her. A fine mist floated down over Milk. It smelt of toilets.

Just then Mrs Blanket spotted Milk. 'Oh look, Malcolm, it's Reecey's little girlfriend.' She reached out and grabbed a handful of Milk's hair. 'Oh dear, your hair looks worse than last time. I do wish you'd let me sort it out. Reecey would be so happy and you do want to please him, don't you?' She jerked Milk's head from side to side as she spoke. 'You know, I do my hair especially for Malcolm every morning, don't I Malky-Moo?'

'Yes,' replied Mr Blanket, somewhat uninterested.

'Do you like my hairstyle?' Mrs Blanket asked Milk. 'It's called a Mermaid's Flunge. I saw it on breakfast television this morning. Apparently *all* the film stars are wearing it. So I had my hairdresser come round toot sweet and fix it up for me. Don't you think it's wonderful?' Milk thought it looked like a curly pile of yellow sick. 'You *must* have a Mermaid's Flunge. We'd be like sisters! I'll call my hairdresser right now.' She finally let go of Milk's hair and rummaged in her bag for her phone.

There were a thousand things that Milk wanted to say to this woman, none of them nice. But she was in a hurry. 'I've got to go. I'm late for school,' was all she managed to splutter.

'Oh, silly me. School! Yes, of course. Reecey's been studying for his test all weekend. He's such a delightful boy. You're a lucky girl, you know!'

And at that Milk pushed her way back through the crowd and ran home to change.

CHAPTER 18

THE TEST

The moment Ms Cerise sashayed into the classroom, Milk put up her hand.

'Yes, Milk? What is it? Some shabby excuse why you haven't done your reading, I suppose.'

'No, Ms Cerise. Not at all.'

'Well, what is it then?'

'I wanted to apologise. For my behaviour last time.'

It was a rare thing to see Ms Cerise lost for words. Slowly and deliberately, she opened her desk drawer and took out her glasses, the ones she'd once stolen from an optician. Without putting them on, she held the glasses up to her eyes and stared hard at Milk.

'I just had to make sure it was the same Milk that was here last week,' she said, sarcastically. 'Well, let's hear you. This should be interesting.'

Milk swallowed hard and tried her best to look remorseful. 'I'm sorry, Ms Cerise, for not listening to you in class last

Friday. It was wrong and from now on I'll do my best to be good.' Then Milk addressed her classmates. 'And I'm sorry that my bad behaviour ruined your weekend.' She paused. Her heart was beating wildly in her chest. It wasn't too late to sit down right now and leave it at that. But she had come this far. She was determined to see her plan through. She took a deep breath and continued. 'And by way of apology I've made chocolate flapjacks for everyone. You too, Ms Cerise. Would it be all right if I handed them out?'

Ms Cerise eyed Milk suspiciously. Years of teaching had made her naturally distrustful of all her pupils. However, Ms Cerise was also a bit of a glutton and the thought of a chocolate flapjack made her thin lips quiver.

Eventually she said, 'Don't think for a minute that this will have any bearing on the test I'm about to give you.'

'Of course it won't, Ms Cerise.'

'I will still make your life as miserable as possible if you, or any of you, fail.'

'I understand, Ms Cerise.'

'In that case, you have my permission to hand them out.'

Milk tried not to look elated as she opened the lid of the Tupperware she had prepared the previous evening. She went up and down the classroom, carefully handing out the miniature chocolate flapjacks to everyone in the classroom, making sure she gave the two biggest ones to Reece and Ms Cerise. Once that was done she returned to her desk at the back of the classroom.

For a moment, the only sound in the classroom was one of contented chewing. Milk had to admit they tasted even better than she hoped. The chocolate topping Jarvis had made was delicious and easily masked any hint of mouldysweetness beneath. He was a good cook after all.

'Right class,' announced Ms Cerise, sweeping the crumbs off her desk, 'it's time for our little test.' She opened her briefcase and pulled out a pile of papers. 'If you've done your reading then these questions should be easy. Melanie Spoons, you could do with the exercise. Hand these out.'

Melanie Spoons did as she was told, placing a test paper on every desk.

Ms Cerise checked her watch. 'You have half an hour from . . . now.'

Milk took out her pencil and pretended to start work. Resting her head in her hands, she peeked through her open fingers, spying on her classmates. Melanie Spoons was looking worried. Fenella Frat was chewing the end of her pencil, not writing anything down. A thin, nervous boy called Jack Pittwoman looked around, almost on the point of tears. Milk crossed her fingers for luck and waited.

Then she saw her first shudder. It was Frank Frat. He seemed momentarily confused, as if he'd just woken up in a strange place. Then he looked down at his test paper and began scribbling away at top speed. Melanie Spoons was next, followed by Jack Pittwoman, both shuddering, just a little, before putting their heads down and getting on with their work. One by one, everyone else in the classroom, apart from Reece Blanket and Ms Cerise, had a little shudder. At last Milk had her own shudder and started the test.

Question 1. Train driver Jenny has a cold. If her train leaves Swindon station at 07:46 and travels at an average speed of 47 miles per hour, at what time will her tissues run out?

It was easy. She wrote down the answer on her test paper.

Question 2. Fat Bob is allergic to prawns. He weighs 102 kilos. Using the Baile Theorem discussed in Chapter 3, calculate the number of prawns he needs to eat before he is violently sick. (Show your workings.)

Just then Ms Cerise spotted Frank Frat looking out of the window. 'You! Frat boy! Why have you stopped working?'

Of all the children in her class, Ms Cerise loved picking on Frank or Fenella Frat the most. They were the perfect pupils; silent, obedient and scared.

Today, however, things were going to be different.

Frank Frat sat up straight, looked Ms Cerise directly in the eye and announced in a clear voice, 'I've finished.'

Ms Cerise froze. She looked like she'd seen a ghost. Frank Frat never spoke! Eventually, she stuttered, 'What did you say?'

'I've finished, Miss. Would you like to check my answers?' replied Frank, calmly wiping his nose on his sleeve. (Some things never change.)

'Are you trying to make a fool of me, boy?' roared Ms Cerise. 'Is this some kind of joke?'

'Not at all, Miss. I've finished the test, that's all.'

'Well, we'll see about that. Bring it to me.'

Frank Frat was not a tall boy. Everybody knew that. With hunched shoulders and a premature stoop, he resembled a worried old man. Yet now, as he crossed the classroom, he seemed ten feet tall. His back was straight and his shoulders pointed to the ceiling. And strangest of all, he was smiling.

'What are you smirking at?' growled Ms Cerise as Frank handed over his paper.

'I'm not smirking, Miss. I'm smiling.'

'Well, don't. It makes you look constipated.'

'Yes, Miss,' replied Frank, still smiling.

And with that, Ms Cerise took out her red pen (yes, it was stolen too), and prepared to mark his paper. Oh, she was going to enjoy putting this boy in his place . . .

But slowly, her expression changed from a sadistic grin to utter confusion. He had got every answer correct.

'You cheated! You must have cheated,' she bellowed, flinging Frank's paper onto the floor.

Frank Frat looked genuinely hurt. 'Not at all, Miss. I studied all weekend, as you asked, and it was really difficult and I didn't think I understood it, but I must have because I found the test really easy.'

Ms Cerise gripped the sides of her desk with her fingers. Such was her fury, the tips of her fingernails sank into the wood. 'Don't lie to me,' she howled. 'Tell me, how did you do it?'

But before Frank could answer, Melanie Spoons announced, 'Miss, I've finished too.'

'And me,' added Jack Pittwoman.

'It was easy, Miss,' chirped Fenella Frat.

One by one, everyone in the class put up their hand and said they were finished. Everyone, that is, apart from Reece Blanket.

It was truly wonderful to watch Ms Cerise, the malicious, spiteful, cruel kleptomaniac, struggling to understand what was going on. This was *her* classroom, where *she* decided what miseries to inflict. Yet, in front of her eyes, her pupils were making her look very stupid.

She slammed her pen down on the desk, splattering red ink on her blouse. 'This isn't possible,' she raged. 'Bring your papers to the front.'

She marked every paper there and then. Her red pen hovered, but not once did she use it; there were no mistakes. The porridge had worked its magic.

In Ms Cerise's mind there was only one possible explanation. 'Somebody must have seen the test and given out the answers. Who was it? Who's the cheat?' She scanned the classroom, looking for a culprit. Inevitably, her eyes stopped on Milk.

'I don't suppose you know anything about this, do you?' she sneered, accusingly.

'No, Ms Cerise. How could I?'

'Maybe you broke into my house and copied the test. Children from broken homes are always doing that sort of thing.'

'I don't even know where you live,' replied Milk, in all honesty. 'And my home isn't broken either.'

'Well, what is your explanation for this outbreak of . . . *cleverity*?'

'Maybe we're cleverer than you think,' suggested Milk.

'Ha!' boomed Ms Cerise. 'With the exception of dear Reece, you lot are about as clever as a brick.'

'But Reece is the only one who hasn't finished the test,' replied Milk.

'Well, that proves it,' declared Ms Cerise, getting to her feet. 'Reece is the only one who *didn't* cheat. Isn't that right, Reece?'

Up until now Reece had remained unusually quiet. He was still stuck on question one. 'Yes, Miss. They must have all cheated,' he agreed wholeheartedly.

That instant, the classroom filled with angry, high-pitched voices.

'That's not true,' insisted Melanie Spoons, going red with fury.

'He's lying,' yelled Jack Pittwoman, who never yelled.

Even Fenella Frat got to her feet and squeaked, 'I'm not a cheat,' over and over.

Ms Cerise walloped her copy of Syd Thicke's *Advanced Maths for Really Clever People* on her desk and demanded silence. But no one was listening to her any more.

Milk leant back in her chair, wallowing in the classroom chaos she had created. This was beyond her wildest dreams. At best, she'd imagined that her classmates would do well in the test and Ms Cerise would be slightly annoyed. But this! This was wonderful!

And then, fuelled by the porridge, Milk had an excellent idea. She stood up and raised her hands, calling for quiet. Gradually her classmates returned to their desks. Milk had become their leader.

'Ms Cerise,' she said calmly. 'Ask us anything you like.'

'What?' quivered Ms Cerise. 'What are you talking about?'

'If you think that we're not very clever, why don't you test us? Ask us anything you like. It'll prove we didn't cheat. And if we give you one wrong answer, then you can punish us any way you like. Detentions, extra homework, anything.'

'And if you answer them all correctly?'

'Then you apologise for calling us cheats.'

'And I can ask you anything I like?' asked Ms Cerise, negotiating the finer points of the deal.

'Anything,' replied Milk, sitting back down.

How can I possibly lose? Ms Cerise asked herself. *I know millions of things. Things they've never even heard of. I'll squash them. I'll make their lives a misery, especially that odious Milk.*

'OK then,' Ms Cerise said, rubbing her hands together, 'let's see what you bunch of snivelling cheats can do.'

CHAPTER 19

JARVIS FINDS HIS FLUSH

Jarvis felt huge. He reached down and patted his enormous stomach that sprawled across the kitchen floor. It was like someone had stuffed an overinflated balloon under his shirt while he was sleeping. With a groan, he rolled onto his back and lifted his head out of the bottom of the fridge. A dollop of blancmange slid down the side of his face.

Slowly he began to piece together the events of the previous day. He had eaten. Lots and lots. And then he'd eaten some more.

He stretched his tongue out of the side of his mouth and licked the blancmange off his cheek. The soft dessert swilled around his mouth, but it tasted of nothing. He was back to normal. No taste buds. The effects of the Porridge of Knowledge had worn off.

Pushing his hands against the floor, he heaved himself into a sitting position. His stomach sank down and flopped onto his lap. When he was little, he would sometimes sit like this on the kitchen floor and watch his mother at work. By all accounts her cooking was exquisite. Everybody said so and the café was always busy. Sometimes Jarvis would help out, chopping this or stirring that, 'to learn the ropes', as his mother used to say. But as hard as he tried he was never going to be as talented as she was. How could he be? Remember the old saying; a chef without taste buds is like a toilet without a flush.

But now things were going to be different. He'd found his 'flush'.

He struggled to his feet, burped, begged your pardon and went through the beaded curtain into the café. Beneath the counter were the six remaining Tupperwares full of the Porridge of Knowledge. Plenty left. He felt a sudden surge of excitement at what he might achieve. All he wanted was to make his parents proud. To make Carp's Café a success once again.

He opened one of the Tupperwares, scooped out a generous lump of gooey porridge and held it up to his face.

'Well then, my little friend,' he said to the porridge, 'let's see what you can do.'

'I'll do my best,' said Jarvis, pretending to be the porridge.

And he popped it into his mouth. As usual it tasted of nothing. He chewed, swallowed and waited. After a moment's thought, he picked out an extra lump of porridge and popped that into his mouth as well. *Just in case*, he told himself, as his body shuddered gently.

CHAPTER 20

GENIUSES

Poor Ms Cerise. How was she to know she was up against a roomful of geniuses? Poor, poor Ms Cerise. She never stood a chance. Not against the Porridge of Knowledge.

Ms Cerise scanned the classroom. Who shall I choose? she asked herself. Who's the most brainless, the most dim-witted . . .?

Her eyes stopped on Melanie Spoons.

Even without the Porridge of Knowledge this was a bad choice. Melanie Spoons was by far the cleverest girl in the class. Not that Ms Cerise had noticed. In fact, all Ms Cerise had seen was a quiet, overweight girl – an easy target to humiliate.

But today things would be different.

'Stand up, Melanie. Let's have a look at you.'

Melanie Spoons did as she was told. Her chair scraped across the floor behind her.

Ms Cerise looked her up and down. 'Have you lost weight?'

'No, Miss.'

'That's correct. You haven't lost weight,' cackled Ms Cerise. 'At least you've got one question right. Well done.'

At the back, Reece Blanket tittered like a little girl. Melanie Spoons didn't flinch, staring hard at Ms Cerise.

'Let's try something a little harder. Tell me, Melanie, what is the capital city of Australia?'

'Canberra,' shot back Melanie, without a moment's hesitation.

Ms Cerise raised her eyebrows. Though it wasn't a very difficult question, she certainly hadn't expected the girl to give her the right answer.

'Oh, very good,' said Ms Cerise, patronisingly. 'It appears that you have been listening in class after all.'

'I didn't learn it from you, Ms Cerise,' replied Melanie Spoons.

'Not from me?'

'No, Miss.'

'From where then?'

Melanie Spoons rolled back her shoulders. 'I just knew it, that's all. I know all the capital cities.'

Ms Cerise felt slightly unsettled. This wasn't the same Melanie Spoons she loved to tease. This was something very new and Ms Cerise didn't like it one bit.

'In that case, if you know them all, what is the capital city of Ecuador?'

'Quito.'

'Jamaica?'

'Kingston.'

'Kazakhstan?'

'It used to be Almaty, but they changed it to Astana in 1997.'

Ms Cerise's eyes almost bulged out of her head. 'SIDDOWN!' she roared.

'That's not a country, Miss.'

'I know it's not a country. I'm telling you to SIT DOWN.'

'Yes, Miss,' replied Melanie Spoons, with a big smile across her face.

Milk leant back in her chair. Things were going swimmingly.

Ms Cerise felt dizzy. This wasn't how she had pictured it. By now she should be giving them all detentions and extra homework.

'Jack Pittwoman. When was Charles Dickens born?'

'1812, Miss,' replied Jack calmly.

'What day?'

'The seventh of February at 3:15 p.m. It was a Tuesday.'

'Fenella Frat. Give me the square root of two hundred and twenty-five.'

'Fifteen,' squeaked Fenella Frat.

'Milk. What is a dodecahedron?'

'A solid figure with twelve faces.'

'Spell it.'

'I-t,' spelt Milk, cheekily.

'No, you idiot. Spell dodecahedron.'

Of course Milk spelt it perfectly.

And so it went on. Ms Cerise fired question after question at her class and every time, the correct answer pinged right

back at her. Her eyes began to twitch. Little white flecks of spit formed at the corners of her mouth. Her mind was going blank. She couldn't think of any more questions. How do they know all this? It's just not possible.

'Is the test finished, Miss?' asked Milk.

'No, no, no,' Ms Cerise stammered. 'I'm sure I can think of one more question. There must, I must . . . there must be something . . . just give me a minute and I'll . . .'

But she had nothing left. She slumped onto her desk, head in hands.

'Are you going to apologise?' asked Frank Frat.

'For calling us cheats,' added Fenella Frat.

'Say sorry,' demanded Melanie Spoons.

'Apologise,' ordered Milk.

Ms Cerise raised her head. She was whiter than a ghost's sheet. 'I'm . . . I'm . . .'

But she just couldn't say it.

She leapt up, grabbed her coat, the one she'd stolen from the charity shop, and stormed out of the classroom.

CHAPTER 21

QUEUE

The Great Fish Clear-up was well under way. As Milk strolled along the promenade she counted at least forty volunteers, armed with buckets and rubber gloves, clearing the beach of dead fish. It wasn't unusual for the people of Slopp-on-Sea to pull together in a crisis like this. It was in their blood. Their history was littered with stories of great courage and camaraderie. For example, there was the time, over a thousand years ago, when Viking ships were spotted near the coastline. Fearing an attack, a ragtag army of Sloppites stood guard on the beach, armed with nothing more than rolled-up wet towels and mouthfuls of spit, ready to whip-spit-away any Viking who dared come ashore to pillage their village. For three days and three nights they stood guard as the enemy ships drew closer. On the fourth day the Vikings raided the neighbouring village of Pifflemundon, razing it to the ground. The people of Slopp celebrated wildly. Not only had their village been spared, but Pifflemundon was destroyed, which was a bonus because nobody liked them anyhow.*

Further down the beach Milk saw Grandad and Mrs Fozz helping out. Cheerful as ever, Mrs Fozz loaded up a bucket with fish carcasses. Then Grandad carried the bucket up the steps onto the promenade and emptied it into a large wheelie bin. Despite the stinkiness of the job, Grandad seemed to be enjoying himself, singing a made-up song as he worked.

'Mussels and cod went to the gym.
Haddock and plaice fell into the bin.
Sardine and salmon sat on the beach,
Tuna and herring squashed a fat peach.'

All nonsense, but it had Mrs Fozz in fits of giggles. Milk liked watching them work together. They were a good team.

Despite the clean-up, the smell around Slopp was getting worse, lingering like a pungent fog. A coach drove past. Milk looked up at the rows of holidaymakers peering out of the windows. Some of them were holding their noses. All of them looked very unhappy.

Milk decided to go home, get changed into her wellies and help with the clean-up. She didn't get far. As she passed

---

* If you want to read more about Slopp-on-Sea's colourful history, ask your librarian for a copy of *Slopp! Our History in Black and White*. It's a delightful read and every one of its sixteen pages is quite good. Well, it's not bad; just check you're not missing anything on TV first.

Carp's Café she saw something that took her breath away.

It was incredible.

Remarkable.

Unbelievable!

Outside Carp's Café was a line of people, some locals, some holidaymakers, queuing to get in. Queuing! Nobody queued to get into Carp's Café. The food was disgusting; everybody knew that. In the bestselling guidebook *Cafés of England*, the question was asked:

Is this worst café in all of England? The answer is yes. Yes, yes, yes, yes, yes and yes again! The food at Carp's Café is so terrible, be sure to bring your own sick bucket.

Yet here it was, clear as day; a queue! Milk was gobsmacked. She ducked down and forced her way through the crowd into the café. Inside it was rammed; jam-packed; standing room only. Every table was full of happy customers, chatting away, tucking into plates of amazing-looking food. Across the café Milk spotted Irene, clearing plates off a table.

'What's going on?' yelled Milk over the din.

'Thank goodness you're here, Milk. I'm too old to be doing this by myself! We only came in for a cup of tea!'

'Where's Alfred?'

'He's over there, the lazy so-and-so.' She nodded in the direction of the counter. 'He's sat on his bum, sorting out the bills, and I'm doing everything else. Typical Alfred. Here, be a love, take these plates to the kitchen for me.'

Milk picked up the stack of plates and weaved her way through the café towards the counter.

'Did you see that?' cried Alfred.

'What?' asked Milk.

'That man. He just left a ten-pound tip. Said it was the best meal he's ever eaten. I tell you, Milk, it's gone barmy. Utterly barmy! And we only came in for a cup of tea!'

'That's what Irene said,' grinned Milk. 'Is Jarvis in the kitchen?'

'He's been in there all day,' replied Alfred. 'Here, allow me.' And like a doorman at a fancy hotel, he held back the beaded curtain and ushered Milk through.

The kitchen was alive! Pots and pans bubbled on the cooker. On every surface were neat piles of ingredients; nuts, grated cheese, freshly chopped herbs, each one rising up like a tiny colourful pyramid. In the oven, a roast chicken sweated out succulent juices and under the grill, a dozen plump sausages hissed and crackled, spitting out hot fat into the flames.

And in the middle of it all was Jarvis, *chef extraordinaire*. With one hand he whisked a bowl of cream, fluffing it into soft, white peaks, while the other chopped carrots at breathtaking speed. At the same time, he flicked open a cupboard with his foot and kicked a sieve up into the air. As it flew in a perfect arc over his head, he spun around, snatched a saucepan of boiling spaghetti off the cooker, caught the sieve and drained the spaghetti into the sink, all in one fluid movement. Then, without even looking, his hand shot out and grabbed two crumpets just as they popped out of the toaster. Seconds later, they were buttered, topped with smoked salmon, squirted with lemon and sprinkled with cracked black pepper. It was quite a performance.

Normally, when Jarvis cooked, he would drop things, trip over things, burn things. Now he moved through his kitchen with grace and elegance. He was like a ballet dancer, in complete control. Over his chef's whites he wore the 'World's Greatest Cook' apron and, for once, it was true.

'There you are, Milk!' beamed Jarvis as he pirouetted over to the fridge and took out an enormous jelly. 'Could you take these crumpets out to table two? And then please, please, please, could you wash up? I'm running out of clean glasses.'

Milk put her pile of plates down next to the sink and picked up the smoked salmon crumpets. 'How did you get all these people to come here?'

'Cupcakes!' cried Jarvis. 'This morning I baked dozens of cupcakes. They were delicious, if I say so myself.' He kissed his fingers, just to show how delicious they were. 'I took them up the promenade and handed them out to the holidaymakers as they got off the coaches. And they loved them! I told them that if they wanted the best meal of their lives they should come to Carp's Café. And here they all are!'

'You're brilliant!' exclaimed Milk.

'I know,' replied Jarvis without a hint of modesty.

'They won't be happy at Café Smoooth.'

'I know,' said Jarvis again. 'Isn't it wonderful! Now where were we? Crumpets! Oh yes. If you could, Milk. Table two. Thank you.'

And he waltzed back to the cooker to stir his gravy.

CHAPTER 22

CHILDREN CAN BE HORRIBLE

Malcolm Blanket smelt a rat. There was something going on and he didn't like it one little bit. Normally, at this time of day, his café was full of holidaymakers drinking coffee, nibbling cakes, *spending money*. But this afternoon, Café Smoooth was empty – a giant, red-and-white-striped ghost café.

Behind the glistening, stainless-steel counter, five uniformed staff pretended to be busy, all the while watching their boss as he paced up and down in between the empty tables. Even the sad-looking red-and-white-striped dolphin stopped swimming around in its tank, pushing its nose up against the glass to see what was going on.

Just then, the door flew open and a gangly young man scampered into the café. He was dressed just like the other staff members, in a red-and-white-striped apron and matching hat. He skidded to a stop in front of Malcolm Blanket and blabbered, 'Sorryitooksolongmrblanketsiriranalltheway.'

(Which translates as, 'Sorry I took so long, Mr Blanket, sir. I ran all the way,' but he always spoke quickly when he was nervous. And his boss, Mr Blanket, made him very nervous indeed.)

There was something reptilian in the way Malcolm Blanket slowly rotated his head in the direction of the young man – like a lizard being disturbed by an irritating fly. 'Well?' he asked. 'What did you find out? Where are all my customers? And this time, speak s l o w l y.'

The young man took off his hat and stood to attention in front of his boss. 'Well, Mr Blanket, sir, erm, I found out that . . .'

'Too close,' interrupted Malcolm Blanket, closing his eyes.

'I'm sorry, sir?'

'You're standing too close to me. I can smell you.'

Obediently, the gangly youth took a step back. 'Is that better, sir?'

Malcolm Blanket opened his eyes. 'Thank you,' he said, though somehow he still managed to sound quite disgusted. 'Continue.'

'Well, sir, one of the coach drivers told me that this morning, a chubby man dressed as a chef was giving away cupcakes to all the holidaymakers. He said he had one himself and they were delicious, best he'd ever had. Light and fluffy on the inside with a lemon icing that melted in the mouth, sir. And then, Mr Blanket, sir, further along the promenade I saw . . .' Anxiously, he scrunched his hat in his hands, wishing it wasn't him who had to break the bad news. '. . . I saw a queue.'

'A queue?'

'Yes, sir. A queue. Outside Carp's Café. They've all gone to Carp's Café.'

You might think, at a time like this, that Malcolm Blanket would get angry. That he would stamp his foot in fury and rant and rave that Carp's Café was stealing his customers. But he didn't. He just stood there, staring.

'I see,' he said with disturbing calmness. He reached into his pocket, pulled out a coin and gave it to his employee. 'For your good work.'

'I saw that!' screeched Mrs Blanket, bursting into the café. 'Malcolm Blanket, you are the most generous man I know. Giving away our money like that.' Like a blustering elephant in a bright orange dress, she galumphed over to the gangly young man. 'Come on, don't be shy. How much did my hubby give you?'

'1p,' he replied, holding up the miserable coin for her inspection.

'Oh, you lucky thing!' she shrieked. 'I tell you, if I didn't keep an eye on the Blanket purse strings, he'd give the lot away. He's a true philatelist, my Malcolm. Always thinking about others.' She grabbed the young man's cheek and waggled it vigorously. 'You must have made my Malcolm very happy. Are you very happy, Malky-Moo?'

'No,' answered Malcolm, monosyllabically.

'A happy Malky-Moo is a happy Vinnie-Winnie,' tittered Mrs Blanket before finally releasing the young man's bruised cheek. 'Now stop fiddling with your hat and go and get me some cakey-wake. I'm starving. And set a table. We've got company. I bumped into Reecey's adorable little teacher, Ms Cerise, and she's coming for tea. She'll be here in a minute. She's carrying my shopping for me. You won't believe how heavy it is.'

On cue, Ms Cerise pushed her way through the café door dragging dozens of boutique shopping bags behind her.

'Don't drag them, Ms Cerise,' barked Mrs Blanket. 'They're not dogs on a lead, they're designer clothes, you know. That's right, pick them up and bring them here.' Then, with a sad sigh, she turned to her husband. 'Poor Ms Cerise, she tells me she's had a terrible day.'

'Oh?' replied Malcolm Blanket, though he couldn't have been less interested.

'She told me that all her pupils – apart from Reece of course, dear little Reecey, he's such a good boy – all the *other* pupils ganged up on her. Apparently that girl Milk, Reecey's girlfriend, you know, the one who's friends with the chef from Carp's Café, well she was the ringleader. Poor Ms Cerise.'

At the mention of Carp's Café, Malcolm Blanket's ears pricked up. It was the second time in five minutes that Carp's Café had been mentioned. Alarm bells went off in his suspicious mind. He didn't believe in coincidences. Now he really smelt a rat.

'Let me help you with those bags,' he said with sudden courteousness to Ms Cerise. 'Come and sit down and tell me all about it. I'll get us some tea.'

'And cake,' bellowed Mrs Blanket. 'Don't forget the cake!'

Over tea and mountains of cake, Ms Cerise told Mr and Mrs Blanket exactly what had happened that day. She didn't leave out a thing; from Milk's apology and the chocolate flapjacks to the whole class answering every question correctly.

'I couldn't believe it,' sobbed Ms Cerise. 'They knew everything. Really difficult things too. It was . . . impossible.'

'There, there, Ms Cerise,' comforted Mrs Blanket. 'Children can be horrible, can't they?'

Ms Cerise nodded and slurped from her cup of tea. 'I hate them. Especially Milk.'

'And she's got awful hair,' added Mrs Blanket. 'Anyhow, enough about you, look at all my shopping! Isn't it exciting!'

And as Mrs Blanket showed off her purchases, Malcolm Blanket got thinking. His empty café, queues outside Carp's Café, Ms Cerise's genius pupils . . . it was all too strange. Somehow, they were all connected and he was determined to find out how.

CHAPTER 23

ARTHUR CHOOD-BISKIT

Word travelled fast. The following day, a small article appeared on page seven of the local newspaper, the *Slopp Gazette*. Beneath a picture of the Slopp Scouts showing off their award-winning collection of string, the newspaper wrote:

QUEUES AT CARP'S CAFÉ

We have eyewitness reports of up to fifty people queuing outside Carp's Café yesterday afternoon. Norwegian holidaymaker Anders Andersen said, 'I heard the food is incredible, so that is why I am doing the queuing.' Another, Katarzyna Fartuszek from Poland, commented, 'Café? I thought this was queue for toilets. Where are toilets, please?' There were unconfirmed reports of a minor scuffle breaking out when a Frenchman attempted to jump the queue and was given a dead leg. Proprietor Jarvis C. Carp was unavailable for comment.

And this was just the beginning. Over the following weeks, as the queues got longer, Jarvis's reputation spread like wildfire. Celebrity chef Arthur Chood-Biskit was spotted in Carp's Café tucking into a beef Wellington and a Japanese film crew travelled six thousand miles to interview Jarvis about his overnight success. To top it all, the latest edition of *Cafés of England* gave Carp's Café five stars out of five, asking the question:

Is this the best café in all of England? The answer is yes. Yes, yes, yes, yes, yes and yes again! The food at Carp's Café is so delicious, be sure to bring all your friends.

Jarvis loved the attention. He regularly came out of the kitchen in the middle of lunch to wild applause from the customers. Wearing his 'World's Greatest Cook' apron he would bow deeply and sign autographs and share recipe tips with enthusiastic fans. There was even talk of a book deal (*Cook with Carp*) and the possibility of a TV cookery show alongside Arthur Chood-Biskit (*Chood-Biskit and Carp*). It was all going bananas.

Of course neither Milk nor Jarvis told a soul about the Porridge of Knowledge. It was their secret. Milk knew it was selfish not to share, but she was having far too much fun. And besides, if everybody was as clever as she was, then what would be the point of that? She didn't want to be the same as everyone else. Being special was, well, *special*.

And so she fell into a routine. Every morning before school she visited Jarvis at Carp's Café. Together they drank tea and talked about all the wonderful things that were happening to them. Then Jarvis would slice two portions of the Porridge of Knowledge and serve them on the same best plates: the goofy, gooey, royal baby plate for Milk and the donkey plate for Jarvis. As soon as they felt the shudder, Jarvis would disappear into the kitchen and Milk headed off to school.

Ms Cerise was a changed woman. No longer did she make cruel comments about Melanie Spoons's size, nor did she pick on Frank and Fenella Frat for being shy and snotty. Best of all, she didn't give the class any homework. None at all. She didn't dare after the whole Syd Thicke maths test fiasco.

But what Milk didn't know was that Ms Cerise was watching *her*. She had become Malcolm Blanket's spy. Every day, after school, Ms Cerise hurried over to Café Smoooth and reported to Malcolm Blanket what she had seen. 'In my thirty-six years as a teacher I've never seen anything like it. I tell you, Mr Blanket . . .'

'Malcolm. Pleeease, call me Malcolm.'

'Ooooh, thank you, Mr Blanket. I mean, *Malcolm*. Where was I? Oh yes. That horrible Milk girl. She makes my blood boil. I tell you, Mr Blanket, there's something going on. Whatever I ask her, she knows the answer. She knows everything. It's just not natural. She wasn't always like this. Yes, she was a cocky little madam, but I used to have the measure of her. She would do what I told her. But now! Ooooh, I'd like to burst her little bubble so that she disappears into thin air and I never have to see her again. Then I can concentrate on teaching *nice* children like your wonderful son, Mr Blanket.'

And all the while, Malcolm Blanket would sit quietly, nodding his head, topping up her teacup, taking it all in.

'And remind me, Ms Cerise, when did this all start?' he asked, pushing his glasses up his beaky nose.

'A few weeks back. That day I gave my class the test.'

'I see. I see,' he said, looking around his empty café. It was all falling into place. Milk's genius had begun at exactly the same time as Carp's Café's incredible popularity. *Coincidence?* he asked himself. *Ridiculous!*

He knew exactly what to do next.

It was time to become Malcolm Blanket, super-spy.

CHAPTER 24

THE LUCKIEST GIRL IN THE WORLD

It had been the busiest day yet. The moment Irene opened the café door at ten o'clock that morning, the customers flooded in, fighting for seats like a fierce game of musical chairs. Carp's Café had become the most famous café in the country, and people would do anything to get a table.

Everyone had their roles. Alfred took the orders and settled the bills, Irene limped about carrying food to the tables and Jarvis scurried around the kitchen like a dervish, cooking up the most exquisite dishes. Even Grandad dropped by to lend a helping hand, washing up the odd plate and putting it in the bin to dry. After school, Milk put on an apron and helped with the afternoon rush, preparing hot drinks and plating up Jarvis's latest speciality, homemade scones smothered with kumquat butter and stinging-nettle jam.

There were still people waiting in the queue at five o'clock when Irene finally closed the café door and pulled down the blinds. Alfred counted that they had served one hundred and twenty-four customers, most of whom had enjoyed three courses. Exhausted, they all sat down at a table together and drank hot Bovril.

'Incredible,' beamed Jarvis. 'That was incredible. Thank you, everybody.' And they raised their mugs in the air, clinking them together.

Milk couldn't remember feeling so happy, surrounded like this by her family and friends. Carp's Café was thriving, Alfred and Irene were too busy to be arguing and even Grandad seemed to be enjoying himself. Milk hadn't seen him in such high spirits for quite some time – perhaps even since Grandma had died. At times he was like his old self, cheerfully chatting with the customers, even if they didn't always understand what he was babbling on about.

And to think all this had been brought about by the Porridge of Knowledge. Who would have thought that such magic existed in the universe?

Surely, thought Milk, *I am the luckiest girl in the world.*

Just then, as Milk was thanking her lucky stars, Jarvis got up from the table, 'Milk?' he asked, nervously scratching his cheek. 'Can you come with me into the kitchen? I want to show you the, err, thingy I was talking about . . .'

Jarvis was hopeless at being subtle. Something was up. Milk put down her cup and followed Jarvis into the kitchen.

'What's wrong?' she asked.

He opened the cupboard under the sink and took out a Tupperware container. Inside there was just one small piece of porridge. 'This is all we've got left.'

145

Milk couldn't believe it. For no good reason she had imagined that the Porridge of Knowledge would last forever, somehow reproducing like magic.

'Well, we'll have to make some more,' she said, decisively.

'When?' asked Jarvis.

Milk tried to imagine a day without porridge. It was impossible. The thought of Ms Cerise regaining control of the classroom made her stomach churn. There was only one possible answer to Jarvis's question. 'Now. We've got to make it right now. But this time we should double the amount.'

'No, we'll triple it!' trumped Jarvis. His legs began skipping beneath him like an overexcited puppy on a linoleum floor. 'Quick. If I go now I'm sure I'll be able to get the ingredients.'

'And I'll go to the Elephant Stones to get more limpets,' said Milk. 'There'll be just enough time before it gets dark.'

'What about the dandruff?' asked Jarvis, putting on his coat. 'We need dandruff.'

'That's easy,' replied Milk, hurrying over to the beaded curtain. 'Alfred!' she called out. 'Could you come in here please? We need you for a moment.'

CHAPTER 25

CAPTAIN GRANDMAAAARRRR

Milk worked quickly, prising limpets off the rock face and dropping them into a plastic bag. It was even more blustery than usual and the light was fading fast. To top it all the tide was coming in; another ten minutes and she'd be cut off. The thought of spending a long, cold, dark night stranded on the Elephant Stones made her work even faster.

As soon as she'd collected enough large limpets she got to her feet and began making her way back to shore. Normally she skipped from boulder to boulder like a cool-headed mountain goat, but now, squinting into the darkness, she took her time, pausing at the edges, trying to work out the best place to land on the next boulder. There was no moonlight to help her. One false move and she would plunge into the dark, churning sea.

Just then, Milk heard a deep roar, as if a train was hurtling through a tunnel towards her. It seemed to be coming from all directions, getting louder and louder until, with a mighty

CRASH, a giant wave collided against the boulder, sending a wall of water shooting up into the air. Instinctively, Milk dropped to her hands and knees, gripping the jagged rock beneath her. Gallons of icy seawater splashed down all around, soaking her to the skin. Now she was scared. Not only was it almost completely dark, but she was cold and wet and at any moment another wave could easily knock her off the rocks. Though she was a strong swimmer, she didn't fancy her chances being tossed around in the sea at night.

Uncontrollable shivers took over her body. In the distance she could see the street lights of Slopp-on-Sea curving along the promenade. She wished she was back in Carp's Café, in the warmth, cooking up the porridge with Jarvis. She wished Grandad was with her to take her hand and guide her back to the beach, just like he used to. *Keep moving*, she told herself. *I've got to keep moving.* She decided to crawl; best to stay low in case of another giant wave. The jagged surface of the boulder cut into her hands and knees. Salt water stung her eyes and the bag of limpets felt heavy and cumbersome as she dragged it behind her. Inch by inch she shuffled forward. She could just make out the shape of the next boulder. It wasn't far away, not a big jump, but too dark to see what kind of landing she would have. But there was no choice. She had to get off the Elephant Stones as soon as possible.

As she pushed herself up, Milk felt something loose roll under her left hand. It was smooth, about the size of a pencil, with a hard spine running up its length. At first she thought it was just a piece of driftwood, washed onto the rock by the wave, but as she brought it close to her face she saw it was a pocket knife, with a single blade that folded neatly into a wooden handle. Her knife! The one given to her by her grandma, the one she had dropped into the sea when Greasy Reece Blanket had dangled her over the edge.

What are the chances? she thought, as she ran her finger up and down the length of the knife, feeling the words that Grandma had engraved onto the wooden handle. She remembered the last time she had come to the Elephant Stones with Grandma and Grandad. It was near the end of Grandma's life, when she was too frail to be clambering around on the boulders. Instead, she sat on a blanket on the beach and watched as Milk and Grandad scoured the rock pools for tiny fish or the shy crabs that would scuttle away from their windswept shadows. Whenever Milk found something interesting she scooped it up in her bucket and brought it back to the beach for Grandma to inspect.

'What have you got for me this time?' Grandma asked, her eyes sparkling with curiosity. 'Ahhh, it's Blackbeard's tongue,' she said, taking a sea slug out of the bucket. 'They say that if you eat one of these you turn into a fearsome pirate.'

'Really?' asked Milk.

'Really,' insisted Grandma. She held the sea slug close to her pale lips. 'Shall I try?'

And before Milk could answer, Grandma arched her neck back and pretended to drop the sea slug into her mouth. Staring hard at Milk she chewed and chewed on nothing more than air and then swallowed, pulling a face as if the most disgusting thing was slithering down her throat.

All of a sudden, she sat bolt upright and growled in her best pirate burr, 'Aarrrrr! Avast, me hearties! I'm Captain Grandmaaaarrrr.'

Carried by the wind, her wicked laugh echoed across the beach and across the Elephant Stones and all the way out to sea.

The memory flooded through Milk like a bowl of hot soup. Instantly, her teeth stopped chattering and a delicious courage flowed through her body. Grandma was with her, she was sure of it.

Without a second thought, Milk leapt forward, landing perfectly on the next boulder. Though she could barely see her own feet, she zigzagged sure-footedly across the surface of the rock, sidestepping the crevices and the slippery edges. Another leap. Another perfect landing. All around her the wind howled and the sea raged, but Milk kept surging ahead, the knife firmly in her hand, until at last she landed on the final boulder. One more jump and she'd be back on the beach. She peered down into the watery gloom. It was high tide. Seawater lapped just inches from her feet, frothing and gushing like an angry washing machine. It was a massive jump to the shore. In all her life she had never jumped that kind of distance.

Milk took four paces back, took a deep breath and charged. Her front foot powered off the edge of the boulder, flinging her high into the air. It was a spectacular leap, airborne for an age, soaring across the water until she landed on the beach, rolling in the sand.

For a moment she didn't know what to do with herself. She sat on the beach hardly able to believe her luck. Great tears began to roll down her cheeks. Porridge or no porridge, she felt she could achieve anything. Grandma was always with her.

CHAPTER 26

LET'S COOK!

Jarvis was making a head start. He laid out the Porridge of Knowledge ingredients on the kitchen counter in the order they were listed in the book, from the burnt toast, all the way through to the dandruff that Alfred had kindly provided. Then he dug out his most gigantic pot and hauled it up onto the cooker. It stood so tall, even on tiptoes he couldn't reach over the rim. After a moment's thought, he scampered upstairs and brought down a stepladder, positioning it beside the cooker.

Now he was ready to cook . . . just as soon as Milk got back with the limpets.

Patience was not one of Jarvis's strengths. He stood by the café window, peering up and down the dark street, tapping his foot anxiously on the floor.

He tried waiting for her, he really did, but in less than a minute he had gnawed three fingernails right down.

Where are you, Milk?

After two minutes he had pulled a loose thread so far out of his sleeve, his jumper developed a whopping hole in the elbow.

Come on, Milk. Hurry up.

By the third minute, he had drawn sixteen smiley faces on the steamed-up window, but still there was no sign of her.

That's it, he thought, and waddled impatiently back into the kitchen.

Perhaps he should have waited after all; cooking with a stepladder was terrifying. You see, Jarvis didn't like heights. Not one little bit. Sometimes, even the thought of changing a light bulb could bring on a cold, nervous sweat.

Nonetheless, he gripped the bottom of the stepladder, took three deep breaths and began his ascent. Surprisingly, going up wasn't too bad. As long as he looked straight ahead, he felt in control. So far so good. At the top, he quickly tipped

the twenty-four slices of burnt toast into the pot. That's when he looked down. What a mistake! Instantly, his heart began thumping and his legs shook like jelly in an earthquake. The stepladder wobbled precariously beneath him, rattling on the kitchen floor.

'Jarvis! What are you doing?' cried Milk, rushing across the kitchen.

'Oh, thank goodness you're back,' whimpered Jarvis. 'Do something. Please!'

Milk grabbed hold of the bottom of the stepladder and with a few soothing words of encouragement, guided Jarvis through his perilous six-step descent. When his feet finally touched the kitchen floor he whooped with joy, as if he had just conquered Mount Everest.

'Thank you, thank you,' he gushed. 'It was tough up there. For a while I didn't think I was going to make it.'

'You were very brave,' said Milk, with a hint of a smile. 'Did you manage to get all the ingredients?'

Jarvis nodded and pointed to the neat piles laid across the kitchen counter. 'I got enough to triple the recipe. How about the limpets?'

Milk showed him her plastic bag, which was still dripping with seawater. 'Well, what are we waiting for? Let's cook!'

Milk stood at the top of the stepladder and stirred the contents of the pot. Before too long, the kitchen filled with the Most Terrible Smell in the World. Even with a tea towel tied firmly over her nose there was no escaping the hideous stink. It permeated right through the tea towel, into her mouth, down her throat, making her stomach retch.

'How's it looking?' asked Jarvis, standing at the bottom of the stepladder.

'Horrible. Just as it should,' replied Milk, trying not to gag. She leant over the edge of the pot and stretched right down inside, stirring everything up good and proper with a wooden spoon. It felt like she was sticking her head into a sulphurous volcano, or worse still, a blocked toilet. For once she wished she had no sense of smell, like Jarvis.

'I think it's ready,' she announced finally, coming up for air. 'Turn off the gas.'

Milk climbed down the stepladder and removed the tea towel from her face.

Her plan had been this: to make the porridge, have a nice cup of tea, then go home and sleep, ready for another day of porridge-fuelled fun. But, instead of saying, 'I'll put the kettle on,' completely different words came out of her mouth.

'Shall we have some porridge?'

Jarvis was as surprised as she was. 'What? Now? It's nearly midnight.'

'Why not? Just to check we made it right.' She couldn't really believe she was suggesting it at all.

Jarvis looked at his friend. The seawater had made her hair stick out in every direction and a small piece of seaweed was still pasted across her cheek.

'OK,' he said with a grin. 'Why not?'

And it was as simple as that. Looking back, Milk sometimes wondered about this moment. Perhaps, she told herself, the fumes of the porridge had overcome her, making her say things that she didn't really mean. Or maybe she was just tired. Who knows? But there was no doubt that this strange little conversation, this brief moment of greed, was to have incredible consequences.

CHAPTER 27

BIG-HEADED

Holding her nose, Milk reached down into the pot and scooped up two wholesome dollops of porridge, splatting them into the plastic bowls that Jarvis held above his head. They took their bowls into the café and sat down. No goofy, gooey, royal baby plate this time. Without cloth napkins or ceremony, they tucked in, washing down the filthy goo with gallons of water.

The shudders came very quickly.

Milk's was first and, this time, it wasn't gentle. Her whole body began shaking so violently she nearly fell off her chair. Jarvis's came immediately after. His head wobbled on his neck and under his jumper his belly quivered like ripples on a pond.

Milk tried to speak. 'W-w-what's h-h-happening?'

'I-I d-d-don't kn-kn-know,' juddered Jarvis.

They both grabbed hold of the table for support. The salt and pepper and plastic tomato danced across the table in a condiment conga, before tumbling off the edge and crashing onto the floor. Milk imagined she was in a rocket, seconds before lift-off, engine roaring, preparing to blast into space.

And then, all of a sudden, it stopped. Milk and Jarvis stared at each other, wide-eyed and woozy.

'Are you OK?' asked Jarvis eventually.

Milk thought long and hard before answering. *Am I OK? Am I OK?* She patted her head, checking it was still attached to her neck. She jiggled her legs and counted her fingers. *Am I OK?* She felt fine. In fact, she was more than fine, she felt great. In fact, she was more than great, she felt exceptional. In fact, she was more than exceptional, she was a . . .

'Genius!' she blurted. 'I'm a genius! Jarvis, I know everything!' Her eyes were glistening like a poodle's wet nose. 'I know that the prime minister picks his nose in bed and wipes it under his pillow. I know that Ms Cerise has nightmares every night about badgers chewing off her fingers. I know where socks go when they disappear from the washing machine. Jarvis, I know everything!'

It was Jarvis's turn to declare his brilliance. 'Well, I know that daddy-long-legs can laugh and if you leave Parmesan cheese in the sun it develops a brain.'

'That's not true,' giggled Milk.

'I know!' screeched Jarvis, clapping his hands.

'Do you realise what this means, Jarvis? We can do anything. We could build a spaceship, or teach llamas to talk, or . . .'

Suddenly she stopped. Jarvis was looking at her in such a strange way. 'What is it? Why are you looking at me like that?'

'Your head,' he mumbled. 'Something's happening to your head.'

'What are you talking about? Don't be silly.'

'No, Milk, look.'

Jarvis picked up a stainless-steel napkin dispenser off a table and held it up to Milk's face.

At first she thought Jarvis was playing a joke, that the curved surface of the napkin dispenser was exaggerating the shape of her head, like those bendy mirrors you get at the funfair.

'Very funny,' she said, pushing the dispenser back towards Jarvis.

'I'm not joking, Milk. Your head is . . . growing.'

And so it was. With every passing second, Milk's head was inflating like a balloon. Her cheeks were getting puffier, her nose was getting wider, her chin was getting longer – her whole head was expanding.

'What's going on?' she cried, touching her ears, which were already the size of plump cauliflowers. 'Jarvis! Do something!'

What do you do when
someone's head is ballooning?
It's not in any first-aid manual:
carpet burns, yes, paper cuts, yes,
stapling your fingers together, yes,
but there's nothing about head
ballooning. So Jarvis did the
only thing he could think
of. He clamped his
hands against
each side
of Milk's
head and
squeezed as
hard as he could.
Instantly, her rubbery
head squished into the most
peculiar hourglass shape, the top
half bulging upwards, eyes popping,
forehead swollen like a camel's hump,
while the bottom half plummeted
down in a flubbery jumble
of mouth and chin.

'Owww!' squealed Milk. 'Stop it!'

Jarvis let go. Instantly, Milk's head pinged out, bigger
than ever, the size of a watermelon and still growing.

In a crisis like this, it is important to remain cool, calm
and collected. Jarvis was none of these. He ran around the

café like a headless chicken, flapping his arms, wailing, 'What shall I do? What shall I do?'

'Go and get help!' bellowed Milk.

'Yes! Of course. We need help,' yelped Jarvis, scampering towards the café door. 'Who shall I get?'

'I don't know!' cried Milk. 'Anyone! Just go!'

'Right. Yes. Anyone!'

But just as he stretched out his hand to open the door, he froze.

'What are you doing?' screeched Milk. 'Don't just stand there!'

'*My* head,' yowled Jarvis, looking at his reflection in the café window. 'It's growing.'

Now Jarvis really panicked. In a desperate attempt to stop the swelling, he reached up and wrapped his arms around his head, interlocking his fingers over the top. But still his head kept growing, getting bigger and bigger, stretching his arms, pushing his elbows out wide. He felt his fingers being wrenched apart, but he didn't let go. He refused to let go. With the top of his head held down, his face grew out. Led by the nose, his eyes and mouth bulged forward in a blubbery protrusion, until his face stuck out like some hideous, undiscovered sea monster.

'Let go of your head,' screamed Milk.

'No!' insisted Jarvis. He felt the tip of his nose pushing against the café window. His fingers were slipping – the pressure was just too great – he couldn't hold on any longer, until, with an almighty *BOING*, his head sprang free.

'Owww!' he yelped, as his head flubbered out, the size of a satellite dish.

It was then Milk realised that something else was happening to them.

They were beginning to float.

'Jarvis, quick! Grab hold of a table,' she cried, taking hold of a table herself.

Jarvis did as he was told, bobbing up and down towards Milk like an astronaut crossing the surface of the moon. He grabbed hold of the other end of her table.

'Not this table!' screamed Milk. 'It's not heavy enough for both of us.'

But it was too late. Already Milk, Jarvis and the table in between them were hovering inches off the ground and rising slowly. Their feet scrambled in mid-air, kicking over chairs and tables. And still they floated, higher and higher, until at last the tops of their heads plumped gently against the café ceiling.

They were stuck, floating twelve feet up, holding a table with a large plastic tomato on it.

'Now what?' whimpered Jarvis, nervously looking down.

Milk looked at the café beneath her. It was strange seeing a place she knew so well from this new, lofty viewpoint. Everything looked so familiar, but at the same time, so completely different. On the counter next to the till she saw the book, *The Porridge of Knowledge* – the book that Grandad had innocently given to her all those weeks ago, the book that had started this wonderful and terrible chain of events. She remembered the day she had read it out loud to Grandad in their kitchen and he had fallen asleep under the newspaper.

Suddenly, a dreadful thought filled her massive head.

'Jarvis,' she said quietly. 'I think we might be in trouble.'

'We're already in trouble.'

'No, you don't understand. Do you remember when I told you about Jim from the *Porridge of Knowledge* book? How in the story he ate too much porridge?'

'Vaguely,' replied Jarvis, eyeing Milk suspiciously. 'Why? What happened to him?'

Milk took a deep breath. 'His head exploded.'

'Exploded?'

If you thought Jarvis was panicking before, that was nothing. Now he really, really panicked. He turned his humongous head towards the door and screamed, 'HELP!' at the top of his voice.

CHAPTER 28

OLIVER AND GEORGE

Malcolm Blanket stood outside Café Smoooth looking up and down the deserted promenade through a pair of binoculars. It was late, and no one was around. Coast clear, he stepped into the middle of the road and signalled into the darkness. Moments later a lorry pulled out of the shadows and came trundling slowly towards him. Its headlights were switched off. On the side of the lorry, in large red-and-white-striped letters, were the words:

CLEAN YOUR TEETH WITH
BLANKET'S TOOTHPASTE.

Underneath was a cartoon picture of a smiling shark, with two rows of sparkling, razor-sharp teeth. In its fin it held a toothbrush and a tube of Blanket's Toothpaste. A speech bubble came out of its mouth. It read:

Steve the Shark says,
'For the best-kept bite, brush with Blanket's.'

Below all that was a black-and-yellow skull and crossbones sticker with the words:

Danger! Toxic Waste. Dispose of Carefully.

The lorry pulled up alongside Café Smoooth, then carefully reversed over the pavement and onto the pier. The wooden flooring groaned and creaked beneath the weight of the lorry. Malcolm Blanket stood behind it, guiding it into a space behind his café. From the road the lorry was completely out of sight.

'Did anyone follow you?' asked Malcolm Blanket.

'No, sir,' replied the driver, a bald, stocky man who seemed to have lost his neck somewhere inside his T-shirt.

'Good. Well, you know the drill. Get to work.'

The driver ducked underneath the lorry, reappearing a moment later with a long, wide hose. He attached one end to the lorry and threw the other end over the pier railings, so it dangled just above the waves.

'It's ready sir. Would you like to press the button or shall I?'

'Of course I push the button,' snapped Malcolm Blanket, slapping the driver's bald head. 'I always get to push the button. It's the best bit.'

On the side of the lorry, hidden among Steve the Shark's teeth, Malcolm Blanket felt for and found a small button.

He pushed it. A gentle whirring sound, no louder than a vacuum cleaner, started up.

The driver leant over the railings and looked down towards the end of the hose. 'Here it comes, sir.'

A vile, bright yellow, sloppy, steaming stream of goo began pumping out of the hose and plopping into the sea. Malcolm Blanket stood beside the driver, watching the sea turn a putrid beige.

'Do you know how much money this saves me?' He didn't wait for the driver to answer. 'A fortune. It would cost thousands to dispose of this through the proper channels. And it's only a few harmless chemicals from my toothpaste factory. Much easier this way, don't you think?' he said, pulling out a crumpled five-pound note from his pocket and handing it to the driver.

'Don't you ever worry about the fish, sir?' pondered the driver, pocketing the money.

'Oh, fish, fish, fish, fish, fish. Why does everyone keep bleating on about the fish?' snarled Malcolm Blanket. 'Do the fish pay your wages? No! Do fish do anything except swim about all day eating other fish? No! They're useless. Who cares about the fish? You're as bad as everybody else around here moaning about the dead fish.'

The driver scratched his bald head and said, 'It's just that I've got two goldfish at home. They're called Oliver and George, and I sometimes wonder if their brothers and sisters are out there somewhere.'

'Oh, for goodness' sake.' Malcolm Blanket had heard enough. 'Get on with your work, you pathetic idiot.' And with that, he marched back onto the promenade to make sure no nosy Sloppites were poking their beaks into his business.

All was quiet. A brisk wind ruffled his hair as he scoured the promenade for busybodies. But it was well after midnight. Of course everyone was in bed. A warm, smug feeling washed over him. He felt very pleased with himself that he was going to get away with it – again – and no one in Slopp-on-Sea would be any the wiser.

Just then, carried on the wind, he heard a strange cry. *Probably a fox*, he told himself. *Nothing to worry about*.

There it was again, louder this time, almost human, like a cry for help. He raised the binoculars to his eyes and scoured the promenade.

That's when he saw lights coming from inside Carp's Café.

Curiosity got the better of him. Malcolm Blanket went to investigate.

CHAPTER 29

A WOLF IN SHEEP'S CLOTHING

On a cold January morning in 1892 Barnabas Blanket wheeled his rickety handcart into an east London market. He had invented a Powder for the Cleansing of Ladies' Teeth, and he intended to make his fortune. The other market traders, their teeth blackened by soot and ale, laughed at his new invention. Who in their right mind would want to have clean teeth? Nevertheless, slowly but surely, his mixture of elderflower, powdered mouse brains and mint caught on. Bad-breathed, slime-toothed Victorian ladies flocked to his stall and by the end of the year he was selling more than he could make. He built a factory, employed fifty men and grew enormous sideburns. Blanket's Toothpaste was born.

As a boy, Malcolm Blanket never wanted to go into toothpaste. For him, the business started by his great-grandfather was a source of enormous embarrassment. The children at school used to call him 'paste-face' or

'Malcolm Talcum', because his teeth were as blindingly white as talcum powder. As a result, young Malcolm learnt never to smile. He became withdrawn, secretive and sly. He imagined that one day he would become a great spy, and he would wreak revenge on his unkind classmates. Of course he never did, and at eighteen he dutifully joined the family business selling toothpaste.

But to this day, to this very moment, he still liked to think of himself as a daring spy. As he made his way up the promenade towards Carp's Café he ducked in and out of shadows, lurking behind lampposts. At the abandoned tennis court, he stopped. With his back pressed against the fence he looked through the binoculars to make sure he hadn't been followed. Nothing. He was still a great spy.

He crawled the final few yards on his hands and knees until, at last, he was crouched beneath the window of Carp's Café. Slowly, silently, he raised his head and peered in.

As far as he could see, the café was empty. But something wasn't right. Across the café floor were upturned tables and chairs, as if there had been some kind of struggle. It was the kind of mystery that Malcolm Blanket, super-spy, couldn't resist. On the count of 007, he pushed open the door.

'We're up here.'

Malcolm Blanket looked up. His mouth fell open. He thought he was prepared for anything, but the sight of two people with gigantic heads, bobbing against the ceiling, holding a table in between them – well, it took his breath away.

'What happened?' he spluttered.

Instantly, Jarvis blabbed, the words spilling out of his mouth at a hundred miles an hour. 'Oh Mr Blanket thank goodness you're here we need help we ate too much porridge and our heads grew so much and we floated up to the ceiling and now our heads might explode and you have to get us to hospital as soon as possible . . .'

'Porridge?' asked Malcolm Blanket. 'What porridge?'

Jarvis was giving too much away. Milk tried kicking him under the table, but her leg swished harmlessly through the air.

'Yes Mr Blanket it's called the Porridge of Knowledge from the book that Milk found and there's a recipe in it that makes you the cleverest person in the world and that's how I became a brilliant chef and we ate too much and now we're in no end of trouble will you help us please because our heads might explode and—'

'Of course I'll help,' interrupted Malcolm Blanket. He

171

adjusted his facial features into what he imagined to be a sympathetic expression. 'Don't panic. I'll look after you. I'll get you to the hospital straight away.' On the surface, he remained calm and collected, but inside he was jumping for joy. He couldn't believe his luck. Without any effort he had discovered the secret of their success. On top of that, Milk and Jarvis were completely at his mercy, just how he liked his rivals to be.

And then a wicked plan entered his head. 'Do you have any string?' he asked innocently.

'In the drawer under the till,' replied Jarvis. 'Why?'

But Malcolm Blanket didn't answer. He made his way around the counter and began rummaging through the drawer.

Milk thought quickly. Though she was pleased there was someone there to help them, she wished it was anybody but Malcolm Blanket. She remembered her grandma telling her once, 'Beware of wolves in sheep's clothing,' and that was certainly true of Malcolm Blanket – she didn't trust him one little bit. On the other hand she also remembered her grandad saying, 'Good things come in strange packages.' Maybe Malcolm Blanket was a good thing in a strange package. Maybe he would help them after all. And they certainly needed help.

'Got it,' said Malcolm Blanket triumphantly, holding up a ball of string. As he came back round the counter, he noticed a book sitting beside the till. His eyes flicked over it, quickly reading the faded gold letters that ran along the spine . . .

His heart, if he really had one, skipped a beat. *This is all too easy*, he said to himself, *like taking candy from big-headed, floating babies.*

But first he had a job to do. He picked up an overturned table, positioned it directly underneath Milk and Jarvis and climbed up onto it. On tiptoes, he could just reach their dangling legs.

'What are you going to do?' asked Milk.

'You'll see,' he replied in a comforting voice. 'Don't worry about a thing. Now, tell me if this is too tight.'

Expertly, he tied a knot around one of Milk's feet. Then, feeding the string through his fingers, he shuffled along the table and tied another knot around Jarvis's foot, before jumping down onto the floor.

Like a child with a balloon, he gave the trailing string a tug, gently pulling their heads away from the ceiling.

'How does that feel?' he asked.

It felt good. It had been very uncomfortable head-squashed against the ceiling.

Malcolm Blanket put the second part of his plan into action. 'My car's outside,' he lied. 'You can both squeeze in and I'll drive you to Pifflemundon Hospital. They can take it from there.' He looked up at them, curled back his lips and attempted a smile. 'Don't worry about a thing. You're in safe hands now.'

Jarvis was relieved. 'Oh, thank you, Mr Blanket. You've been so kind.'

Milk was less sure, but what choice did she have?

Malcolm Blanket got to work. Standing directly beneath the table, he pulled on the string. It took some effort – he was hardly a strong man – but inch by inch Milk, Jarvis and the table began to descend. When the bottom of the table was almost touching his head, Malcolm Blanket opened his mouth, put the string in between his magnificent teeth and clamped down hard. With his hands now free, he reached up and grabbed each side of the table, pulling it down so it appeared to be balancing on his head. For all the world, they resembled a bizarre circus act.

With Jarvis's legs dangling in front of him, and Milk's behind him, Malcolm Blanket turned towards the open café door.

'Do you think our heads will go through?' asked Jarvis, nervously eyeing up the narrow exit.

Malcolm Blanket spat the string out of his mouth. 'Of course your heads will go through. There's plenty of room.'

'They won't,' insisted Milk. 'Maybe you should get some help. Call an ambulance or something.'

But Malcolm Blanket didn't want to wait for an ambulance. He wanted this over as soon as possible. Nor did he want any witnesses. Without another word, he charged.

Jarvis yelped as his head smacked against the door frame. His neck stretched and pulled, his ears scrunched against the jambs, until at last his head sprang free on the other side.

'I'm through!' he yelled.

It was Milk's turn. She ducked her head down and closed her eyes. Her bulbous head squished square-shaped as it plugged the door frame. She felt like she was being dragged face-first down a rabbit hole. Jarvis screamed encouragement. 'Go on, Milk! Push it! You can do it, Milk!'

And then, with one final thrust, she was through! She opened her eyes. Across the table she saw Jarvis grinning wildly at her. They'd made it. They were going to be all right.

'Thank you, Mr Blanket,' said Milk, peering down under the table. 'It was a bit of a squeeze but you were right. Now, which one's your car?'

Malcolm Blanket was quite out of breath. Eventually he turned and looked up at Milk. 'What car?' he asked.

'Your car. To take us to hospital.'

'But I don't have a car, I can't even drive,' he said with a smirk. 'Anyhow, surely it'd be quicker if you flew to the hospital.'

And with that he let go of the table.

'What are you doing?' screamed Milk, as she and Jarvis began floating up into the sky. 'Grab the string!'

But he didn't. The ball of string began unravelling at his feet, spinning and jumping on the ground, getting smaller and smaller until there was almost nothing left.

At the last second, Malcolm Blanket's hand shot out and grabbed the very end of the trailing string just as it floated up in front of him.

'Phew! That was close,' he teased.

He arched his head back and gave them a little wave. 'This is fun,' he said, yanking the string. 'It's like flying a kite. Are you having fun up there?'

'No. Pull us down. Now!' demanded Milk. She stretched out an arm and tried to grab hold of the café roof.

'Temper, temper,' chided Malcolm Blanket. 'Didn't anybody tell you it's not safe for little girls to be climbing about on roofs?' With a quick tug of the string he jerked Milk's outstretched arm away from the roof. 'Actually, I never much saw the point of kites. I'd much rather read a good book. Expand the mind. You don't have a book I can borrow, do you? What about . . . what's it called, *The Porridge of Knowledge*? I saw it in the café. You don't mind if I borrow it? I've heard it's mind-blowing.'

And with that he let go of the string.

Milk, Jarvis and the table in between them drifted up and away, into the Slopp-on-Sea night sky.

CHAPTER 30

FISH FOOD

'Don't let go of the table, whatever you do,' said Milk firmly. 'Jarvis? Did you hear me?'

Jarvis managed to nod his huge head, but his eyes remained tightly closed. Six steps up a stepladder was bad enough; floating over the village was, to put it mildly, very, very bad indeed.

'If we let go of the table, we'll float even higher. Just don't let go.' Perhaps she shouldn't have mentioned the bit about going higher, because Jarvis began whimpering like a tuneless mouse.

The wind seemed to come from all directions, buffeting them one way then the other. Wild gusts sent them plummeting towards the ground, then threw them back up again, higher than ever. Milk looked down. Spread out beneath her was a zigzag world of rooftops, broken tiles and chimney stacks. There were TV aerials sprouting up like spiky plants from another planet and across one flat

roof, a playful cat chased after the trailing string, leaping up, trying to catch it with its paws.

'Grab it!' Milk yelled, without really thinking what she was saying. It was, after all, only a cat.

The cat stopped and stared up at her with bright, curious eyes, as if to say, 'Yeah right! I'm a cat. What am I supposed to do?'

All of a sudden Milk realised they were floating over her street. And there was her house! She could see the bell hanging outside her front door and the windows of her bedroom.

'Grandad!' she roared at the top of her voice. 'It's Milk. Help! Anyone. Mrs Fozz. Mrs Farley. Mr Fub! Wake up!'

She waited for a light to come on. She hoped and prayed for someone to open a window or step out into the street. But nobody did. It was the middle of the night and everyone was fast asleep. In desperation, Milk grabbed the plastic tomato off the table and flung it as hard as she could in the direction of the bell. If she hit it, surely the clang would wake someone up. But it missed by miles, splattering against a window some way down the street.

Once again the wind changed direction. 'Hold on!' cried Milk as they rocked and rolled in the turbulent sky. Their massive heads acted like sails, catching the wind, driving them across the promenade and over the sea. Things were looking bad. She knew Jarvis couldn't swim. If their heads started shrinking and they floated down into the water they would be in no end of trouble. In a gruesome way, it would be better if their heads exploded after all. At least it would be quick. They would become fish food.

Despite the wind, the sea looked very calm. Along the shoreline, she saw hundreds of tiny, glimmering silver objects rolling back and forth in the surf. At first she thought it was the reflection of the promenade lights flickering on the water. But as she squinted down she realised they were fish: dead fish. Beyond them, a streak of yellow cut through the darkness of the sea, running in a current all the way back to the pier. That's when she saw the lorry, with a hose sticking out of the side, spewing out vile, yellow muck. Even from this height, she could read the words on the side of the lorry:

CLEAN YOUR TEETH WITH
BLANKET'S TOOTHPASTE.

So that was it! Malcolm Blanket was polluting the water. The people of Slopp would wake up in the morning and find their beach covered in dead fish all over again. Some time later Milk and Jarvis would be reported missing. And all because of Malcolm Blanket. Milk was furious. She beat her fist so hard on the table that Jarvis actually opened his eyes for the first time. He took one look around him and squealed, before quickly shutting them again.

'Milk,' he stuttered. 'We're . . .'

'I know,' replied Milk.

They were drifting out to sea.

CHAPTER 31

UNIDENTIFIED FLOATING OBJECT

There was an almighty *SPLAT* against the window. Fenella Frat shot up in bed.

'What was that?' she whispered, turning on her bedside light. 'Frank, did you hear that?'

'Yeah,' replied Frank. His frightened eyes were the size of conkers.

'Open the curtains and have a look.'

'Why me? You go.'

'What if it's vampires?' asked Fenella.

Frank wiped his nose on his pyjama sleeve. She had a point. 'Let's both go.'

They got out of bed and tiptoed across the room. Slowly, Fenella pulled back the curtain just enough to peek through.

'Blood!' wailed Frank, staggering back.

The windowpane was splattered with a thick, red pulp, which dribbled and glooped down the glass.

'That's not blood,' said Fenella. 'Look.'

On the windowsill sat a large plastic tomato, lying on its side. The lid had come off and sauce oozed out of the opening.

Fenella opened the window, bent down and took a sniff. 'It's ketchup.'

'Where did it come from?' asked Frank, braver now. He leant out of the window and peered up and down the street. It was empty. Across the road he saw a cat sitting on a roof, staring into the sky. Frank followed the cat's gaze. That's when he saw, well, *something*, floating towards the promenade.

'Fen, look,' he said, pointing up. 'What is it?'

Fenella stretched out of the window and squinted into the sky. 'I dunno. Quick, get your telescope.'

For his birthday, Mr and Mrs Frat had given Frank a telescope. Not a proper telescope for looking at the stars, but a small plastic toy with a skull and crossbones sticker peeling off the end, to give it a piratey feel. It was rubbish really, and if the truth be told, Mrs Frat had found it washed up on the beach.

Frank opened the telescope and pointed it in the direction of the unidentified floating object.

'I'm not really sure,' he said, adjusting the focus. 'It looks like a table and two balloons with legs and string hanging down. Maybe it's a kite or something.'

'Let me have a look,' said Fenella, snatching the telescope off her brother.

She was quiet for a moment as she stared into the toy. Then, turning to Frank, she whispered, 'They're massive!'

'What's massive?'

'Their heads!'

'Whose heads?' asked Frank, thoroughly confused.

'Come on,' said Fenella. 'We'd better hurry. Milk's in trouble.'

They didn't bother getting dressed. Downstairs, the television was on, some programme about kittens that kill. In front of it, Mr and Mrs Frat were snoring, fast asleep on the sofa.

Quiet as mice, Frank and Fenella tiptoed along the hallway, opened the front door and stepped out onto the street.

'Maybe we should get some help,' suggested Frank.

Fenella agreed, so they pitter-pattered barefoot up the street and knocked on Grandad's door. No one answered. Fenella pointed at the large brass bell that hung outside the house.

'But you'll wake everybody up,' worried Frank.

'That's the point. It's an emergency.' And she reached up and rang the bell – three hefty clangs.

Grandad was the first to come out. He was in his pyjamas with his snoozing cat curled around his bald head like a Cossack's hat.

'Am I missing?' he asked.

'No, it's Milk. She's needs help. And Mr Carp too,' explained Fenella hurriedly.

Nice Mrs Farley popped her head out of the door. 'Oh dear, is he missing?' she asked, pulling her dressing gown around her.

Grandad scratched his head, which was actually the cat's head. 'Yes, I'm missing. I don't know where I am.'

'But you're there,' said Mrs Farley, pointing at him.

'Well, that's a relief. I thought I was missing,' replied Grandad, perfectly reasonably.

Mr Fub stepped out onto the street, rubbing sleepy dust out of his eyes. 'Aren't you supposed to be missing?' he said to Grandad.

'I'm not sure. Shall I go?'

Frank and Fenella tried to get everyone's attention, but the three elderly people were having quite a debate. To add to the matter, Mrs Fozz came outside. She wore a long, flowing nightdress, with matching sleeping cap.

'Oooh, isn't this nice! Are we going rat catching?' she asked. 'Where's Grandad?'

'I'm not here. I'm missing.'

'Oh dear, that's a shame. Frank and Fenella, what are you doing up? Would you like a banana? I've got some inside. They're a bit green though.'

'Or some cake?' added Mrs Farley.

Suddenly, in a voice louder than she knew she had, Fenella Frat yelled, 'Everybody! Please listen!'

'There's no need to shout,' grumbled Mr Fub.

Quickly, Fenella explained what she had seen out of her window.

'They need our help,' added Frank. 'Right away.'

'Well, what are we waiting for?' asked Mrs Fozz, waving her sleeping cap around her head. 'Let's go.'

'Maybe we'll find Grandad on the way,' said Grandad hopefully.

And so the raggle-taggle rescue party set off down the hill towards the promenade. They hadn't got far when Mr and Mrs Frat marched onto the pavement, blocking their way.

'Who's been ringing that stupid bell? It's three o'clock in the stupid morning,' raged Mrs Frat.

'I was trying to watch *Kittens That Kill*,' added Mr Frat, scratching his bum.

Just then Mrs Frat noticed her children. 'Frank!' she roared. 'Fenella!' she growled. 'What are you doing out with this demented lot? Get back inside this instant.'

Frank and Fenella Frat didn't budge.

'Did you hear what your mother said? Get back inside,' fumed Mr Frat.

'But Milk needs our help,' said Frank. He could hear his voice shaking. He had never stood up to his parents before.

'Well, I might have known,' spat Mrs Frat. 'Whenever there's trouble that Milk girl's name always comes up. Why she was never sent to an orphanage in the first place is beyond me.'

'She might die,' whispered Fenella.

'I couldn't care less. Now get in, the pair of you. Hanging about with a bunch of dribbling oldies in the middle of the night. It's embarrassing. What will the neighbours think?'

It had been years since Grandad had spoken much sense. No one expected much more than befuddled gobbledygook to come out of his mouth. However, as he pushed his way in between Frank and Fenella, he addressed Mr Frat in a cool, calm voice. 'Milk is my granddaughter. Frank and Fenella tell me she's in trouble. They're coming with us to help. Now stand aside.'

'Or what, you old fool?' snarled Mr Frat, squaring up to Grandad.

In one swift movement, Grandad whipped the plastic telescope out of Frank's hand and whacked Mr Frat around the head.

'Ow!' he squealed. 'What did you do that for?'

Grandad whacked him again, this time on his freshly scratched bum.

'Ow! Get off me.'

'Good shot!' giggled Mrs Fozz.

'He's gone barmy,' wailed Mrs Frat.

'I'm already barmy,' warbled Grandad. 'We're all barmy. Come on, everyone.' And with that, he marched off down the street with his barmy army following behind.

'Frank! Fenella! Come back now,' screeched Mrs Frat.

But this time they didn't listen.

CHAPTER 32

MR FERRIS

Heads back, mouths open, the raggle-taggle-barmy-army stared up into the sky.

'There they are!' shrieked Mrs Fozz, who had forgotten to bring her glasses with her.

'No, Mrs Fozz. That's a lamppost,' said Mr Fub.

Fenella scanned the night sky with the plastic pirate telescope. There was no moon; out to sea was one giant expanse of darkness. They could be anywhere.

'I can see them!' yelped Mrs Fozz, jumping up and down with excitement.

'No, Mrs Fozz. It's a seagull,' said Mr Fub patiently.

'Maybe they floated down onto the beach,' suggested Frank.

He crossed the road and stood on the promenade wall. That's when he saw the dead fish, rolling back and forth in the surf. 'Everybody! Look!' he called out.

They all came to see. Mrs Farley could hardly hold back the tears. 'It's so sad. All those poor fish. Why's it happening again?'

But Grandad had other things on his mind. 'Forget the fish,' he pleaded. 'Where's Milk?'

Just then, out of the corner of her fuzzy eye, Mrs Fozz saw something floating in the sky. 'Look, Mr Fub! Over there.'

Mr Fub was about to tell her to go home and get her glasses when he too saw what she was pointing at. 'Fenella, take a look over there.'

Fenella swung the telescope in the direction of the pier. 'It's them!' she squealed. 'Quick, hurry!'

Despite their age, the four oldies moved surprisingly fast. It was quite a sight. In a flurry of dressing gowns and pyjamas and cat hats they dawdleflipped along the promenade, reaching the entrance to the pier in no time at all.

'Come on,' cried Frank, leading the way. He ran through the open gates and started up the pier.

They weaved their way past the long-abandoned attractions: the rusty old bumper cars, the not-so-scary ghost train and the merry-go-round that hadn't gone round, neither merrily nor miserably, in over fifty years. At the end of the pier stood the enormous, three hundred-foot-tall Ferris wheel. It was once the pride of Slopp-on-Sea (and the envy of Pifflemundon), but now the empty carriages swung back and forth in the wind, creaking like an old man's bones.

'Can you see them?' asked a breathless Mrs Fozz. Her nightcap flapped about in the wind, slapping her cheeks.

They all stared into the darkness, straining to catch a glimpse of Milk and Jarvis.

'There they are,' pointed Frank.

There they were indeed, some way out to sea. The wind hurled them one way then another. In the blink of an eye they plummeted towards the frothing water, skimming the waves, before shooting up again, dangerously high.

'What shall we do?' asked Fenella.

'We should spread out,' suggested Mr Fub. 'We'll have a better chance of catching them if they come close to the pier.'

It was a good idea. They all scattered themselves around the end of the pier, all, that is, except for Grandad, who stayed where he was, fiddling about at the base of the Ferris wheel. He opened a large wooden lid and leant so far in that his legs dangled up in the air.

'What he's doing?' yelled Frank to his sister.

Fenella shrugged her shoulders.

But Mrs Fozz knew exactly what Grandad was doing. She remembered as a young girl visiting the pier and riding the Ferris wheel with her mother and father. She remembered the young man who helped operate it. He wasn't called Grandad then – everyone knew him as Mr Ferris.

'He's trying to fix it! Mr Ferris is trying to fix it!' she squealed.

'But it's impossible. It hasn't worked for fifty years,' said Mr Fub.

'If anyone can do it, he can.'

Suddenly, a magnificent rumble shook the pier and, like a giant waking up after a long sleep, the Ferris wheel began turning.

'It's going!' screeched Mrs Fozz over the creaks and groans of the wheel. 'You're a genius, Mr Ferris. A genius!'

Grandad stepped back and watched the Ferris wheel turning. Then, with an enormous smile, he flicked a switch and a thousand lights spluttered to life all around the wheel.

'Jarvis,' cried Milk. 'Look!'

'I can't,' shivered Jarvis, keeping his eyes screwed up tight.

'No. It's something good. It's wonderful. Look!'

Reluctantly, Jarvis opened one eye. 'What is it?'

'Over there! The Ferris wheel.'

For a moment, Jarvis forgot where he was. The Ferris wheel lit up the night sky like a glorious multicoloured sun.

'And there are people on it. I can see them, Jarvis. They're waving at us. They're trying to help us.'

'But how can we get to them? We haven't got a sail. We've got nothing.'

Of course! It was obvious! 'Jarvis, you're brilliant!'

'What have I done?'

'Quick, tilt the table. We can use it as a sail. It might just work.'

The moment they tilted the table, the wind caught behind it, blasting them towards the pier.

'It's working!' screeched Milk. 'Hold it steady!'

They raced through the sky at terrific speed, twisting the table to adjust their course. The turbulence pummelled their huge rubbery faces.

Now Milk could see their rescuers. On the Ferris wheel were Mr Fub, Frank and Mrs Fozz, while Fenella, Mrs Farley and Grandad waited on the pier.

'Jarvis! Listen to me. On three, we're going to let go of the table. Are you ready? One, two, three!'

The table dropped away into the sea. Instantly, their speed decreased and they glided effortlessly towards the top of the Ferris wheel. Mrs Fozz stood up in her seat and stretched out towards them.

'Got you!' she screamed, grabbing hold of Jarvis's ankle.

Jarvis had never felt so relieved in all his life. Big, fat tears sprang from his eyes and rolled down his overinflated cheeks. 'Oh thank you, thank you. Don't let go. Please don't let go.'

'Don't you worry,' said Mrs Fozz, holding on tight. 'You're not going anywhere now.'

CHAPTER 33

THE WET BLANKET

There was a lot of explaining to do. Under the light of the Ferris wheel, Milk started at the beginning, from the day Grandad gave her the book, through the ants and the cows, right up to the moment Malcolm Blanket tricked them, releasing them into the sky.

'But this is Slopp-on-Sea,' insisted nice Mrs Farley. 'Nothing like that ever happens around here. That's why I live in Slopp. If I wanted excitement like that I'd move to Swindon.'

Mrs Fozz and Mr Fub both nodded their heads in agreement.

'I never meant for any of this to happen,' said Milk, touching her big head. 'Thank you, everybody. If it wasn't for all of you, Jarvis and I, well . . .' She didn't know what else to say, so she gave Grandad a big hug instead.

'What about your heads? Will they stay like that?' asked Fenella, pushing an exploratory finger into Milk's puffy cheek.

But already Milk had noticed that Jarvis's head wasn't quite as big as before. It looked like it was slowly shrinking. Maybe their heads wouldn't explode after all. Maybe they wouldn't become fish food.

Suddenly Milk froze. 'Fish!' she exclaimed. 'We know who's been poisoning the fish. We saw a lorry pumping something horrible into the sea. It's got something to do with Malcolm Blanket and his toothpaste company, I'm sure of it.'

'Why, that good-for-nothing so-and-so,' fumed Mrs Fozz. 'If he was here right now I'd put him over my knee and give him a good spanking.'

'Quick. If we hurry, the lorry might still be there. We can catch him in the act.' Milk tried to set off back down the pier, but with her head still inflated she just hovered, legs scampering uselessly through the air.

'Let me help,' said Frank Frat, taking Milk's hand. 'I'll pull you.'

Milk blushed, but accepted his hand nonetheless.

Just then, a voice came from beyond the pier. 'Oh, you hussy! Not so long ago you were my Reecey's little girlfriend.'

Lavinia Blanket stood on the deck of the *Wet Blanket* as it cruised slowly around the end of the pier. She wore a sailor's cap with the words *Captain's Wife* emblazoned across the front. 'And look at your head. Malcolm said it was big, but that is something else! Reecey, quick! Come and look at her monstrous head!'

Reece Blanket came up on deck. He wore a sailor's cap with the words *Captain's Son* emblazoned across the front.

He took one look at Milk and began sniggering like a hyena. 'That's disgusting,' he said in between snorts. 'You look funny. Where's my camera, Mummy? I want to remember this when we're in the Bahamas.'

'It'll take more than a Mermaid's Plunge to cover that head,' declared Lavinia Blanket. 'You'll need a proper wig. Oh, and look at the chubby chef,' she added, noticing Jarvis. 'And to think I thought you handsome when we first met. Now look at you. You look like a weather balloon!'

As the *Wet Blanket* eased around the pier, Malcolm Blanket came into view. He stood proudly behind the steering wheel wearing a sailor's cap with the words *Captain Blanket* emblazoned across the front. He gestured up at the illuminated Ferris wheel. 'A farewell party? How thoughtful of you.'

Mrs Fozz rushed over to the railings and yelled, 'We know you've been poisoning the fish! Come back here now! You won't get away with it!'

Malcolm Blanket looked genuinely irritated. 'I wish everyone would stop bleating on about the fish. Ugly, bony things they are. Save the whale? What for?!'

'You are a very nasty man indeed,' said nice Mrs Farley, which was about as rude as she had ever been to anyone.

'True, true,' acknowledged Malcolm Blanket. 'And soon I'll be a very clever man as well. The cleverest in the world, didn't you say?' He picked up *The Porridge of Knowledge* and flicked through the pages. 'Looks like an interesting read. Oh, and there's a recipe in the back,' he added, with mock surprise. 'I'll have to try it when I get to the Bahamas.'

'Give that back,' shouted Milk. 'It's mine.'

'Finders keepers,' he said, steering the boat out to sea. 'Well, we must be off now. We won't be back for a very long time. I'll instruct my staff at Café Smoooth to give you all half-price cupcakes any time you drop by. My little parting gesture. Lavinia, Reece, wave goodbye to the nice people.'

'Bye bye, Milk,' snorted Reece. 'I'll send you a postcard.'

'And sort your hair out. Please!' added Lavinia Blanket. 'You could be so pretty if only you tried. Byeeeeee.'

And with that, Malcolm Blanket revved the powerful engine and the *Wet Blanket* glided away into the night sea.

CHAPTER 34

WHIRLPOOL

They all went back to Carp's Café for a cup of fishy tea. It was Mrs Fozz's idea, 'to celebrate the successful rescue of Milk and Jarvis', though no one particularly felt like celebrating. The mood was sombre. Malcolm Blanket had got away with it and there was nothing they could do.

Nobody paid much attention when Grandad came through from the kitchen munching a flapjack. He sat down at the table, dunked it into his fishy tea and took another bite, chewing methodically like a dozy cow.

'Grandad?' asked Milk suspiciously. 'Where did you get that flapjack?'

'What jackflap?' asked Grandad.

'The one you're eating.'

Grandad held the flapjack up to his face and studied it for a moment. He was about to say something when he shuddered, just a little, but it was a definite shudder.

In crystal-clear, unbefuddled words, he answered, 'I found

it in a Tupperware box in the cupboard under the kitchen sink. It was the last one. I hope you don't mind.'

'Grandad,' said Milk as calmly as she could, 'that wasn't a flapjack. It was porridge. You're eating the Porridge of Knowledge!'

Everyone looked up from their cups of tea and stared at Grandad.

'I thought it tasted a bit funny,' he said, grinning wildly. 'How exciting! Does this mean I'm clever?'

'You're very clever,' said Jarvis.

'Fancy that! I've always wanted to be clever.'

'Don't eat any more,' said Milk, quickly whisking the last mouthful out of his hand. 'I don't want your head exploding.'

With the cat still snoozing on his head, Grandad got to his feet and rubbed his hands together. 'Well, what are we waiting for?'

'What do you mean?' asked Frank Frat.

'While we sit here drinking Jarvis's fine tea, Malcolm Blanket is getting away.'

'He's long gone,' grumbled Mr Fub. 'There's nothing we can do.'

'Nothing?' asked Grandad, with a twinkle in his eye. 'Are you sure?'

'But we don't have a boat,' added Fenella. 'And even if we did, we'd never be able to catch him.'

'Who said anything about a boat?'

Milk looked up at him. It was strange but wonderful seeing him like this. He was his old playful self once again. She felt like she was five years old.

'Grandad, you're teasing us. Have you got an idea?'

'Of course I have!' he giggled. 'I'm clever, remember!'

Under Grandad's instruction, they all went through to the kitchen and tried lifting the enormous pot of porridge off the cooker. But it was no good. Five strong men would have struggled to lift it, let alone the assembled crew of geriatrics, children and bigheads. It was just too heavy.

Grandad had a think. All eyes were on him to come up with a solution. It didn't take long.

He picked up a fork off the kitchen counter and pointed it at the big heads. 'Milk, Jarvis, you two float up and hold the pot by the handles. The rest of you lift from underneath.'

Everyone got into position.

'Ready? OK. Heave!'

This time, with Milk and Jarvis acting like overhead cranes, the pot slid off the cooker and onto the others' shoulders. Knees buckled and elderly bones creaked, but still they held on.

'What now?' wheezed Mr Fub.

'To the beach,' declared Grandad.

'The beach?'

'Yup. I fancy a swim.'

With tiny steps, they shuffled through the beaded curtains, across the café and out onto the street. The porridge pot swayed and wobbled but somehow didn't fall, even when Mrs Farley's dressing gown blew open, revealing a remarkable pair of bedtime bloomers.

'Nearly there,' encouraged Grandad, as they negotiated the steps down onto the pebbled beach. 'Just a bit further now. There. Now, put it down.'

With a collective sigh of relief they lowered the pot onto the pebbles.

The beach was like a battlefield. There were dead and dying fish everywhere, some floating in the sea, others on the pebbles, mouths opening and closing. On top of this Milk saw turtles and crabs and jellyfish and even one or two seabirds washing back and forth in the surf. It was carnage.

Grandad put his plan into action. To the blushes of Mrs Farley (and the giggles of Mrs Fozz) he stripped down to his underpants and carefully removed the cat from his head, passing it to Mr Fub. Then, he took hold of the pot and dragged it over the pebbles towards the sea.

'What's he doing?' asked Frank.

Milk shrugged, though not for a moment did she doubt him. She knew all too well the power of the porridge.

Dawn was breaking over Slopp-on-Sea. The black, starless sky turned charcoal, shifting through shades of grey, before settling on a less-than-thrilling sludgey colour. By Slopp standards, it was going to be a beautiful day.

Grandad stood waist-deep in the water, pointing with the fork towards a boat-like speck on the horizon. 'I see them,' he growled in his best pirate burr. 'If all goes to plan, the Blankets are going to get quite a surprise.' He turned and grinned at his raggle-taggle-barmy-army on the beach. 'Ladies and Gentlemen,' he announced, 'sit back, relax and enjoy the show.'

With a mighty heave, he tipped the porridge pot over into the water. It lay there, submerged like a shipwreck, with just the side curving above the waves. Clumps of porridge began floating up to the surface, mingling with the dying fish. Grandad dived down and swam inside the pot. Using the fork, he scratched at the porridge stuck to the bottom, swishing it out into the sea behind him.

At last, his age-speckled bald head emerged from the water. 'Come on, fishy fish,' he said under his breath. 'Eat up your porridge.'

He wiped the salt water out of his eyes and waited.

It's hard to see fish shudder. But they did.

Fenella was the first to notice it; around Grandad's head, a small shoal of fish began swimming in a tight circle, mouth to tail.

'What are they doing?' she asked, getting to her feet. 'Why are they swimming like that?'

As the porridge drifted further out into the water, more and more fish joined the shoal, swimming in the same circular pattern. It grew bigger by the second, quickly expanding into one gigantic spiral of fish. Soon it was as wide as a house.

Grandad watched with glee. 'Come on, my beauties. That's it, swim! Swim! SWIM!'

The fish responded. They swam faster and faster around his head, spinning at such ferocious speed they formed a whirlpool, sucking the water up off the seabed. Slowly but surely, the sea drew back until Grandad, the old man of the sea, was completely surrounded by a revolving wall of water.

It was then Milk realised what was happening. 'They know!' she squealed. 'The fish know who poisoned them.'

'How do they know?' asked Frank.

'Because of the porridge!'

Suddenly, Grandad leapt up and pointed out towards the open sea. 'GO!' he roared, holding the fork aloft like a bald-headed Neptune. And they did! On his command, millions of fish shot out into the sea towards the *Wet Blanket* on the horizon.

'I've got to see this,' said Milk, getting to her feet. Her head was almost back to a normal size, but she wasn't about to take any chances. 'Frank, Fenella, take my hands.'

'Where are we going?' asked Fenella.

'To watch the show.'

With Milk bobbing gently in between them, the three children hurried back up the steps and along the promenade.

'This is the one,' said Milk, stopping in front of her coin-operated telescope. She felt beneath the tube of the telescope and found her 20p, as ever, stuck there with old chewing gum. She peeled the gum off the coin and dropped it into the slot. There was a gentle *click* as the telescope activated.

It didn't take long to find the shoal of fish. Even from a distance it was huge, shooting through the water like a dark shadow. Further on the horizon Milk could see the outline of the *Wet Blanket*. It wouldn't be long now.

'Can I see?' asked Frank.

Milk stepped aside.

'Wow!' he cried. 'They're moving fast. They're getting closer. They're nearly there.'

'My turn, my turn,' pleaded Fenella, who was jumping up and down with excitement. Frank stepped aside and let his sister have a look. 'I can see them! They've caught up with the boat. They're swimming around it. Fast! Really fast! The boat's turning. Milk, you've got to see this.'

Milk put her eye against the telescope. 'It's a whirlpool! It's incredible. The boat's spinning so fast . . .'

Suddenly the telescope clicked and the view through the telescope went black.

Quick as she could, Milk opened the coin box underneath the telescope, retrieved her 20p and put it back in the slot.

'What can you see?' asked Frank hurriedly.

Milk squinted into the telescope and scanned the horizon. But there was nothing to see. The boat was gone. The fish had gone. The sea was calm.

'It's gone,' said Milk, turning to Frank and Fenella.

'What do you mean, gone?' asked Frank.

'I mean it's gone. There's no boat.'

'What do you think happened?' asked Fenella, wiping her nose on her pyjama sleeve.

'Who cares! Good riddance, is what I say,' said Frank firmly.

Milk and Fenella nodded in agreement.

'Come on,' said Milk. 'Let's go and tell the others.'

And hand in hand in hand they set off back towards the beach.

CHAPTER 35

PIPE AND SLIPPERS

With long, lolloping, flat-footed strides, shoulders slightly hunched and arms dangling by his sides, Grandad wandered along the promenade. He stopped to talk to a wheelie bin, remarking that yes, it was unusually warm for this time of year, before wishing it a good afternoon and continuing his walk. Outside Carp's Café he lingered for a moment, peering in through the window. As usual, it was empty apart from Alfred and Irene who shared a single cup of fishy tea. They appeared to be bickering about something – Alfred, looking cross, waving his arms above his head and Irene poking him in his ribs with her walking stick.

Further along the promenade, Grandad sat down on a bench. Next to him was a discarded copy of the *Slopp Gazette*. If he had looked at it he would have seen the headline:

POLICE ARREST LOCAL TEACHER CAUGHT
STEALING FROM CHARITY SHOP,

but he was far too busy, enthralled by an ant that was crawling along the top of the bench carrying a breadcrumb twice its size.

'Hello, ant,' said Grandad.

'Hello, Grandad,' replied the ant, who was somewhat out of breath.

They chit-chatted for a while about the weather, football, colony overpopulation, that kind of thing, before Grandad got up, wished the ant a good afternoon and went on his way.

It started to rain, so Grandad decided to walk along the beach. The smooth pebbles felt good under his slippers. He remembered the day Grandma had given them to him. She had joked that he was an old man now and next birthday she'd give him a pipe to go with the slippers. But she didn't live long enough to give him the pipe.

'I'll buy *myself* a pipe,' he said out loud. 'That's what I'll do.'

He missed her terribly, but tried not to think about it too much; besides, he still had Milk to look after. Dear, wonderful Milk.

He found two things on the beach that afternoon. The first was a large piece of driftwood that would be perfect for the next bonfire he had in his garden. Thanking his lucky stars, he picked up one end of the driftwood and began dragging it along the beach.

The other thing he found was much less exciting. Rolling back and forth in the surf was a thin red book, the size of a postcard. Along the spine of the book, in faded gold letters, was written:

THE PORRIDGE OF KNOWLEDGE.

Its hard cover had gone soft from the seawater, and the pages were all stuck together in one great clump, but, he supposed, with a little care, it would dry out well enough. He had a thought to show it to Milk. Perhaps she would find some use for it.

He tucked the book into his coat pocket and headed home.

Acknowledgements

A gigantic and heartfelt thank you to all my family, especially Mum, in whose house huge dollops of *Porridge* were conceived and written. You made it all possible.

Also, special thanks to Ian, Andy, Elliott and Mellie Mel for all the years of porridge we've shared.

RIP Doonican, the original Jumblecat.

About the Author

Ever since reading 'sodium monofluorophosphate' on the side of a toothpaste tube, Archie Kimpton has enjoyed putting words together and seeing what comes out. He graduated from Manchester University in 1991 and spent the next twenty years in preparation for his moment of authordom – flogging salami, script writing, book binding and care working in the interim. *The Porridge of Knowledge* is his second novel. His debut, *Jumblecat*, was published in 2014. He lives in South London with his wife and kids. Follow Archie at www.archiekimpton.wordpress.com or on Twitter: @ArchieKimpton.

About the Illustrator

Kate Hindley lives and works in Birmingham (near the chocolate factory). She studied illustration at Falmouth College of Art, and went on to work for two years as a children's print designer at a studio in Northampton, while working on children's books and greetings cards. She has exhibited with her good chums Girls Who Draw and Inkygoodness across the UK, and had a jolly good time painting up a totem pole for the Pictoplasma Character Walk exhibition in 2011. Things Kate finds inspiring include Bob Godfrey, Richard Scarry, *The Magic Roundabout* (in particular, Dougal and the Blue Cat) and Sharp's Doom Bar. Kate's first picture book, *The Great Snorkle Hunt*, written by Claire Freedman, was published by Simon & Schuster in August 2013 and was longlisted for the 2013 Kate Greenaway Medal. *The Porridge of Knowledge* is her second collaboration with Archie Kimpton; her first, *Jumblecat*, was published in 2014. Follow Kate at www.katehindley.com or on Twitter: @hindleyillos.

Thank you for choosing a Hot Key book.

If you want to know more about our authors and what we publish, you can find us online.

You can start at our website

www.hotkeybooks.com

And you can also find us on:

We hope to see you soon!